THE SCARS DON'T SHOW

MICHAEL BRADY SHORT READS 1

MARK RICHARDS

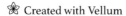 Created with Vellum

AUTHOR'S NOTE

Welcome to the first book in the Michael Brady Short Reads series.

Michael Brady first appeared in *Salt in the Wounds*, set in Whitby in 2015.

The Scars Don't Show takes you back to the start of his career as a detective. He's in Greater Manchester Police – and desperate to prove himself...

Each of the Short Reads is around a third the length of a normal book. They're books that you can read in an evening. They're the stories that trace Brady's career. That made him the detective he is today...

As I'm British and my books are set in the UK, I've used British English. The dialogue is realistic for the characters, which means they occasionally swear.

This is a work of fiction. All names, characters, organisations, some places, events and incidents are either products of the author's imagination or used fictionally. All the characters in this book are fictitious. Any resemblance to actual persons, living or dead, is purely coincidental.

www.markrichards.co.uk

DECEMBER 1998: THE NATIVITY PLAY

The first snowflakes of the winter drifted lazily down as Sarah Cooke reversed her car out of the drive.

She smiled. Perfect. Just perfect. Not enough snow to make driving difficult: enough to make everything magical.

Especially for the nativity play. Especially if your little girl was the Angel Gabriel. If you were walking across the school playground afterwards. Holding her hand as the light faded, the snowflakes swirling and dancing in the streetlights. Telling her for the hundredth time how many sleeps there were until Santa came.

Saying, '*Of course* Santa knows how good you were in the play. *Of course* he was watching...'

Sarah glanced up into the rear view mirror. Braked. Gave the mother pushing her pram plenty of time. Waved into the mirror in case she glanced at the car.

Took her foot off the brake and gently started reversing.

Heard the explosion.

The glass shattering.

Inches from her head.

Felt something shower her face. Stamped on the brake. Stalled the car. Tasted blood in her mouth. Gripped the steering wheel. Closed her eyes. Forced herself not to scream.

Felt the blood running down her face.

Knew she had to open her eyes.

Knew she had to turn her head and look.

Knew who she would see.

You've got to open your eyes, Sarah. You've got to look through the window.

Her ex-husband.

Standing. Smiling. The garden spade in his right hand.

"It doesn't look much, love. Just cuts. Wanted to get your attention. Glad I caught you."

She was still gripping the steering wheel. Sarah looked down. Saw the blood dripping onto her coat. Knew she had to speak to him.

"Gary. You've smashed my car window. You've put a fucking shovel through my car window."

"Don't swear, Sarah. You know it makes me angry. And the car's nothing. Bring it into the garage in the morning. We'll soon fix it. And it's a spade, sweetheart, not a shovel."

"And what am I supposed to do in the meantime? How the – How am I supposed to collect Sophie from school?"

She was sitting in her car. Having a normal conversation with a man who'd just put a spade –

Spade? Shovel? How stupid of me. What sort of woman doesn't understand the difference between a spade and a shovel?

– through her car window. A man who was standing on her drive, still casually holding the spade. The one with the green handle. The one he must have taken from the garage.

Gary Cooke put his hand in his pocket. Pulled out a roll of £20 notes. Peeled off half a dozen. Thrust the money through the window. "Get a taxi. And take Sophie out for a pizza. We're open at eight in the morning. You know John, don't you? He's always in early. He'll sort you out."

Madness. Beyond madness.

He's never going to let me go.

"Just tell me, Gary. How am I going to explain the cuts to Sophie?"

"Tell her you tripped."

"Right, Gary. 'Mummy tripped and hurt herself.' Almost the first words our daughter learned to say…"

1

"You want some advice, Mike? You want a long and happy career in Greater Manchester Police?"

Michael Brady – 26, looking younger, nearly three years into his police career – handed Ernie Moss – 48, looking 58, counting the days to retirement – the coffee he'd been sent for.

"What advice is that, Sarge?"

"Don't work Christmas Eve. Whatever it takes. 'Flu, Bubonic Plague, saving up every last bit of holiday you have... Don't work Christmas Eve."

"You mean it ruins your relationship?"

Moss looked up from the paperwork he was laboriously completing. "No, son. You can leave that to the other 364 days. *Fairytale of New York*. It's like a cat's bloody chorus in the cells. Now piss off home to that pretty girlfriend of yours, Happy Christmas and I'll see you on Monday morning."

Brady hesitated. "Sarge..."

Moss sighed. "I promise, Mike. The first chance I get

after Christmas. I'll have a word with him. I know you want to be in plain clothes. I've recommended you. The boss agrees with me. But there has to be a vacancy. And he can't conjure one out of thin air. Now for the last time bugger off home and have sex. You'll have children soon enough. Women are funny things. They don't feel that romantic when they've been puked on at three in the morning..."

Thirty minutes later Brady put his key in the front door of a three-bedroomed terrace house in Stockport.

Four weeks. Four weeks today since we moved in...

He walked into the hall and hung his coat up.

"I'm back," he shouted upstairs.

"I'm in bed."

"Five minutes..."

Brady walked through into the kitchen. Opened the fridge and poured himself some orange juice. Decided he was too tired to make a sandwich. Felt a lot less tired when he saw Grace.

She was sitting up in bed reading, wearing one of his old t-shirts, dark brown hair tumbling to her shoulders.

And better looking every time I see her...

"Tough night?" she said.

He shook his head. "Not really. About the same as a Saturday night. Teenagers making the most of their fake IDs. Girls who can barely stand wanting a Christmas kiss."

Grace raised her eyebrows. "Come and get into bed, PC Brady. I'm not drunk but..."

Brady shook his head. "Give me ten minutes. I need a shower first. I've been arresting drunks all night. I need to wash it off me."

He unbuttoned his shirt and threw it in the laundry basket. "What time are we at your parents' tomorrow?"

"Twelve-ish?"

"Are we sleeping in your old bedroom?"

"*I'm* sleeping in my old bedroom. You know how strait-laced my mother is."

"Bloody hell, Grace, we've bought a house. We're getting married next year. Does she think we sleep in separate bedrooms?"

"I can't change her, Mike. It's only for two nights."

"I'll creep along the corridor in the middle of the night."

"The floorboards creak. Now get undressed. I want to see *Police Magazine's* Arse of the Year. And don't waste time in the shower. You're not the only one that thinks two days is a long time..."

2

"You want to walk down to the pub, Mike? Half an hour while Val and Grace are getting dinner ready?"

Not really, no. Because after last night I don't want a drink. And you're going to ask me if I'm still in uniform. And you're going to ever-so-subtly suggest that your only daughter could have done better...

"If Valerie's alright with it, George. You're sure there's nothing I can do to help?"

"We're better off out of the way. Come on, G&T, time for a chat and then come back and carve the turkey."

Michael Brady walked into the kitchen, kissed Grace, hopefully asked if there was "anything *at all* I can do to help" – and reached reluctantly for his coat.

"YOU'RE STILL in uniform then, Mike?" Brady's future father-in-law said as they walked back from the Horseshoes.

"At the moment..."

"No sign of you getting into plain clothes any time soon?"

"I've been on the course," Brady said. "I've passed all my exams. My name's gone forward. Now I'm waiting for a vacancy…"

"You don't want – " George Miller broke off to wave at someone in a BMW he'd been chatting to in the pub. Who, just on what Brady had seen in the half-an-hour that had become an hour, must be well over the limit. "You don't want me to put a word in for you? I play golf with Charlie Broadbent. Chief Constable? Can't do any harm."

"No, really. I appreciate what you're saying, George – and I'm grateful. But – "

But having a word with the Chief Constable won't do any good because he hasn't got a clue who I am. And if I'm going to get into plain clothes I'm going to do it on my own. And there's already enough bitching about wet-behind-the-ears graduates being fast-tracked…

"But you want to do it on your own? Well, I admire that in you. I just wonder if you made the right career choice, Mike? We've a young lad in the office. Paul Naylor. You might know him? Graduated at the same time as you. Sharp boy, very ambitious. He'll be a partner in five or six years."

They were back. They scrunched across the gravel and through the front door. George was lightly scolded by a wife who clearly knew from experience what 'just walking down to the pub for half an hour' really meant. Brady didn't get off so lightly. "You stink of smoke,

Michael. Go and have a wash. And change your shirt. And be quick. Dinner's ready…"

IF HIS FATHER had drilled one thing into him, it was saying thank you. Brady handed his future mother-in-law the flowers – an early morning walk to the village shop – and kissed her on the cheek. "Thanks, Valerie. We've had a lovely Christmas. Thank you for everything."

"It's been lovely having you, Mike. You take good care of my girl, won't you?"

He shook hands with George – "Think about the discussion we had, Mike. I only want what's best for you." "I will, George. I promise" – and climbed into the car.

"Remember to wave," Grace said as she slid in next to him.

Brady dutifully waved. And hoped Grace didn't notice the sigh of relief as he drove off the gravel and onto the country lane.

"You alright?" she said, five minutes later.

"Yeah, I'm fine. Glad to be going home." He looked across at her, reached out and put his hand on her thigh. "I've missed you."

"I've missed you too," she said, putting his hand back on the steering wheel. "But not on the M56. Concentrate on your driving, my love. There's…" Grace hesitated. "There's something I need to tell you. It's good news. Sort of. But you won't think so."

"This sounds ominous. What is it?"

"Mum gave me a cheque. She said… Don't get cross, Mike. She said we had to buy a new settee."

You're going to regret saying it. But you're going to say it anyway.

"Bloody hell, Grace, we're saving up for a settee. You know that."

"I do. But she said, when she came round... And you have to admit, Mike, that settee from your old flat isn't... Well, it isn't *Ideal Home* is it?"

"But it was going to be *our* settee, Grace. Now it'll be your bloody mother's settee."

And she'll turn up every fortnight to inspect it...

"You're taking it the wrong way, Mike."

"No, I'm not, Grace. It's our house. *Our* furniture."

"But Mum and Dad can afford it, Mike."

"Right. And they – "

"They what?"

"No, nothing. I don't want to fall out with you. Let's just get home..."

3

"Morning, Sarge. Good Christmas?"

"I ate too much. I held my new grandson. City won away. A bloody excellent Christmas thank you, Mike. Yourself?"

"Grace's parents..."

"Oh." Ernie Moss nodded sympathetically. "Don't say any more. I'll light a candle for you. But..." Moss winked at him. "Get yourself in front of a mirror and straighten your tie. You're wanted upstairs."

"What? I'm on patrol with Eddie Harvey."

"You were. You're not now. Detective Chief Inspector Fitzpatrick would like a word with you. So straighten your tie and two-at-a-time up those stairs. You've been called to God's right hand."

"Sit down," Jim Fitzpatrick said two minutes later.

"Yes, sir."

Fitzpatrick – grey hair combed straight back, worry lines on his forehead, pictures of his grandchildren jostling for a place among the commendations – shook his head.

"Forget the 'sir.' 'Boss' is just fine." Fitzpatrick pulled a file towards him, looked up and smiled. "This is the moment in the movies where I intimidate you. Say I've been going through your file. You think something's wrong..."

Brady knew he was supposed to laugh. Realised he was too nervous.

"Edinburgh University? Why Edinburgh?"

It was the first lesson Brady learned from him. *'The question they don't expect, Mike. Ask the obvious question and they've got the lie ready and waiting.'*

"I was brought up in Whitby, sir. I wanted to go to a city."

"You didn't want to stay up there when you graduated?"

Brady shook his head. "No, sir." *Dare I risk a joke? Too dark? Too cold? No.*

"Why GMP then? Why Manchester? Why not somewhere closer to home?"

"Because GMP offered me a job, sir. You know I went travelling when I graduated – "

"Where did you go?"

"The Far East mostly. I spent three months in Japan. Another three months working in a beach bar in Bali..."

Fitzpatrick laughed. "So you decided the weather wasn't good enough and came back to Manchester?"

"Yes, sir. Sorry, boss. Like I say, I was offered a job. A

couple of forces... I don't know, maybe they thought I'd want to be off again."

And they were suspicious of graduates...

"And you don't?"

"No, boss. I'm getting married next summer. We've bought a house in Stockport."

Jim Fitzpatrick nodded. "So... I've been going through your file. I'm impressed. You might be the first copper I've ever come across who uses semi-colons in a report. But you might just be wasted on Saturday night drunks and RTAs. And... I sense you're frustrated."

I'm clearly supposed to be reply to that.

"I'm just doing – "

"Doing your job? Yes, so was I for about three or four years. I was going out of my mind. By the end of the third year I was wondering if I'd chosen the right career. Exactly like you're doing."

Brady started to reply. Fitzpatrick held his hand up. "On the assumption that you've got a reasonable pair of trousers and a jacket downstairs, go and get changed. And if you haven't got a normal tie go and buy one. Stan Bulman's partner is going to be off for a while. And Bill Slater's taking early retirement. So congratulations Acting-Detective Constable Brady, there's a vacancy. And Ernie Moss keeps nagging me. Unless you've become attached to working Saturday nights?"

This time Brady did laugh. "No, sir. And yes, sir. I mean 'boss.' And yes, I've got a tie."

"Good. Go and get changed. Back here in ten minutes."

4

_____

"Stan? I want you to take Mike Brady out with you this morning."

Stan Bulman looked less than impressed. A lot less than impressed. "Where's Norris, boss?"

"He's severed the tendons in his thumb."

"What? How the hell did he do that?"

Jim Fitzpatrick looked resigned. "I'd like to tell you he did it vaulting over a wall and arresting Manchester's most wanted. Sadly the answer is carving the bloody turkey. I suspect he was pissed in charge of a carving knife. So take young Master Brady with you and teach him the ropes."

"COME ON THEN, Padawan. Investigate this complaint we shall. Complete bollocks it will be."

Brady followed Bulman – balding, overweight, the evidence of yesterday's egg mayonnaise sandwich on his tie – down to the car park. Waited while he unlocked a

Mondeo that would have given even the most battle-hardened valeter sleepless nights.

"Hang on." Bulman reached across to the passenger seat, scooped up a pile of papers and threw them into the back seat.

"You don't mind if I smoke? Well, fuck it. I'm a DS and you're fresh out of college – "

"If four years is 'fresh out of...'"

"Yeah, well, it is in my book. Ten years and you can start to call yourself a copper. What did you do at college anyway?"

"University," Brady said. "And I read law."

"Law? Then you're an idiot. Why didn't you become a solicitor? Nice suits. Fuck off to the pub on Friday lunchtime. Come back at three and shag your secretary."

December or not Brady decided he was going to open the window. Either that or die of smoke inhalation. "I wanted to be a detective," he said simply.

"Right. You're mental. Fucking criminals now, they've no respect. In the old days they accepted they were going to get nicked. Now, you do six weeks' work, you nick someone. Expensive bloody solicitor turns up and gets them off on a technicality. 'Cos we didn't do the bloody paperwork right."

Rumour had it the latest 'technicality' had been Stan Bulman losing some evidence. Brady thought it was probably best to keep quiet.

"Joined the lodge, have you?"

"The Masonic lodge? No."

"Take my word for it, son. Fitz said I should teach you the ropes. Rope number one. You want to get on, join the lodge. Anyway, careers lesson over. We're here. Twenty-three. Nice house. Looks like she did alright out of the divorce."

"The report said her ex-husband – Gary Cooke – had stuck a spade through her car window. Covered her in glass."

"When was that then?"

"Tuesday 15th. She was going to see her daughter in the nativity play."

"Ten days before Christmas? Bloody stupid time to make a complaint. Anyway, it'll be bollocks. I know Gary Cooke. He's a good lad. Done well for himself. She's pissed off that she didn't get enough in the divorce. Stone through the window on the motorway I'd say. But fuck it, we're here. Let's see what she's got to say for herself."

BRADY GUESSED Sarah Cooke was about 30. Three or four years older than him. Long dark hair, hazel eyes, a striking face. A brave smile this morning. Her house an equal mixture of Christmas decorations and scattered toys.

Bulman made the introductions. "And this is Police Constable Brady, who's playing detectives for the day."

Brady shook hands. Looked at her face. More than two weeks ago. Any cuts had healed. Or were hidden under her make up.

Sarah Cooke apologised for the mess. "My daughter's four. I no sooner put the toys away then Sophie gets them out again."

"Is that her?" Brady said.

There was a picture on the bookcase. A little girl in a long white dress. Angel's wings and a cloak. A tinsel halo.

Sarah Cooke nodded. "That's when it happened," she said. "The day of the nativity play."

She offered them coffee. Bulman said that would be fine. "Two sugars. And some chocolate digestives to go with it if you've got any, love."

Coffee in hand, reluctantly conceding that a plain digestive would do, Bulman started asking questions. "You say your ex-husband put a spade through your car window. Is that the car, love? The one outside?"

"Yes. It's the only car I have, obviously."

"It's just that the window doesn't seem to be broken now."

Brady glanced across at Sarah Cooke. She looked resigned, defeated. Knowing from experience where the conversation was going.

"The window was fixed. You're probably aware – "

"That Gary owns a vehicle repair shop? Right. Took my own car in there. Some arse pulling out of a side street. Cracking job they did." Stan Bulman paused. "You see... The problem's this. You've made a complaint. We can't see any evidence of the complaint. There weren't any witnesses, I suppose?"

Sarah shook her head. "No. It happened in the middle of the afternoon. Well, you know that from the complaint."

"And it doesn't make sense, does it? I mean, if someone did what Gary did – what you allege he did... The last thing I'd do is let them fix my car."

"He didn't give me a choice. He's never given me a choice."

"You see," Bulman said. "We're screwed. No evidence, no witnesses." He spread his hands. A very clear 'what can we do?' gesture.

Bulman reached forward and helped himself to another digestive. Sat back and looked around the lounge. "You did alright out of the divorce though. So you can't have fallen out that much."

"I've got a child, detective – "

"Detective Sergeant, if you don't mind, love."

"My child's entitled to a home. I'm entitled to a home."

The pretence of questions carried on for another five minutes. Then Bulman stood up. "I need a wee," he said. "Upstairs is it, love?"

"There's one in the hall."

"No, I like the bathroom. Big bloke like me. Can't squeeze into those bloody tiny bogs."

Sarah reluctantly gave him directions. Bulman plodded upstairs. Brady heard the bathroom door shut. "Did you go to the doctors?" he said. "The hospital?"

She shook her head. "How could I? I had to collect my daughter. Go in a taxi. Tell her that a stone had gone through the car window." She looked at him. "That's what pisses me off. Hitting me, threatening me. Stalking. That's my life. Normal life. What I can't cope with is lying to Sophie. She's five next month. She still believes in Santa Claus. She still believes Mummy tripped and banged her head. She'll stop believing in both of them at the same time. Then what the hell do I do?"

Brady shook his head. "I don't know. I can't – "

"You can't imagine? No. No-one can. They ask you how it happened. Pretend to understand. Then they say, 'But you're an intelligent woman...'

How do you do that to someone? I couldn't imagine. Grace...

She held his gaze. Desperate. Imploring. "Can I have your phone number?"

"Why do you need my number? Bulman's in charge."

"Because I have to tell someone my story. Someone who hasn't made their mind up before they've walked through the door. Here." She passed him a notebook. Looked at him. Pleading.

"I'm not sure I should do that."

"Please..."

Brady took his pen out and wrote his number down.

"Thank you. And no, you probably shouldn't. You're probably breaking all the rules on your first day. But you look like a good person. That sounds silly. I'm sorry."

Brady shook his head. "No. It's fine. I hope so. I try to be."

She flicked her eyes towards the stairs. "Why did you join the police?"

"You mean when it's full of people like DS Bulman?"

"I suppose so, yes."

"Because it's what I always wanted to do. Because – this doesn't sound very fashionable, sorry – I believe in right and wrong."

Bulman banged the bathroom door, walked heavily back downstairs.

"Done here, are we? Not thought of anything else,

love? We'll be off, then. And don't worry. Everything'll be fine. You'll see. Gary's a good lad."

"YOU MIND if I open the window?" Brady said as he climbed back into Bulman's car.

"Smoke too much for you? Give it a couple of years and you'll have joined the rest of us. Marlboro through the day, Macallan at night and hope you make it to your pension. Anyway, what did you make of her? Pretty little thing."

"I thought... I thought her story was believable. The bruises had faded. The cuts had healed. Or they were under make-up. But what she told us... It was consistent with the report."

"So you believed her?"

"On balance, yes. I don't see any reason not to believe her."

Bulman reached in his pocket. Pulled out his packet of Marlboros. Lit one, inhaled deeply.

"You *definitely* believed her?"

"Yes," Brady said.

"Well that's your career fucked, pal. If you're going to believe every tart in a tight pair of jeans. Defence lawyers are going to love you. Like I told her. I know Gary Cooke. He's a good lad. Driven. Ambitious. He likes a drink – but who doesn't?"

Bulman started the car. "Come on, let's get back. See if there's any real work to do. And only a year to wait."

"What for?"

"Millennium Bug, old son. This time next year it'll

have fucked all the computers and we can take the year off."

Bulman turned on to the main road. Took one last drag on his Marlboro and flicked it out of the window. "Let me give you another tip as well," he said. "Three tips."

"What's that?"

"Don't make it personal. You liked her. I could tell. Don't. You let it get personal, you take it home with you. Sooner or later it fucks up your marriage. And your judgement."

"What's the second one?"

"Keep their phone numbers. Everyone. Not just the ones you fancy."

"I didn't – "

"I know. Teasing aren't I? Banter. But keep the numbers. You'll have more contacts than any man has a right to have. Your wife will pick up your phone and think you're having an affair. Ten affairs. But keep the numbers. You think a witness has nothing more to tell you. Something changes – and he's the one person you need to talk to. And fast."

"I will do. And the third one?"

"Always go for a pee. Whether you want one or not. You can tell a lot about someone from their bathroom. Besides, women like Sarah Cooke – " He looked across at Brady and winked. "Nine times out of ten they have their knickers drying in the bathroom."

Brady opened the window wider. Decided it was safer to talk about football.

5

She phoned him on New Year's Eve.

Common sense tapped Brady gently on the shoulder. For the second time in a week he ignored it.

"It's the price I pay for being off at Christmas," he explained. "Four days in a row over New Year."

"Tuesday 5th then? It's Sophie's first day back at school so it's good for me."

It was good for Brady as well. They arranged a time. Brady told Grace to meet him there afterwards. "I'll buy you some lunch."

"You wanted to tell me your story," he said, handing Sarah Cooke a coffee. He took his coat off, held his hand out. "Pass me your coat, I'll hang it up for you."

"Thank you."

"Scarf?"

Sarah Cooke shook her head. "It's not that warm in here. I'll keep it on."

"Thank you for seeing me," she said when Brady had

sat down. "You want to hear my story. I can tell you it in four words... I've made a will."

She saw Brady's look of surprise. Nodded. "I'm thirty years old and I've made a will. Before he does me some serious damage." She stirred her coffee. Looked down into the cup. Looked back up at Brady. "How many women of my age make a will?"

Brady didn't know how to reply. She answered for him. "You're thinking, 'bloody hell that's dramatic.' And you're right. It is. Sitting here, having coffee, Christmas lights, people shopping in the sales, it sounds ridiculous. But I'm frightened. More than frightened. Terrified."

"Can I ask a question?" Brady said. "Before we get into the detail?"

Sarah nodded. "Anything you want. Someone needs to hear the full story. Go ahead."

"I know you said I looked sympathetic. Words to that effect. But why me?"

She looked into his eyes. "Why am I trusting another man? Why not a woman? That's the question you're really asking, isn't it?"

Brady nodded. "Yes, I suppose I am."

"I've spoken to women. In the police. Someone in social services. And you know what? They both asked the same question. You're thinking it as well. 'You're an intelligent woman. Good job.' Well... I did have a good job. 'How can you let that happen to you?'"

"Yes," Brady said. "I was. I'm sorry."

"Don't be. It's hard – almost impossible – to understand. Unless you're in an abusive relationship. And then you know. It just happens. You wake up one morning and you're covered in bruises. And you think 'how did that happen?' Did *he* do that? He can't have done. He's the father of my child. I love him. I thought I loved him. And suddenly you're living in this parallel universe. Because one day he's turned you black and blue and the next he's standing there with a bunch of roses and he's bought tickets for the theatre and this funny, challenging, ambitious man you fell in love with is back."

"Can we go back to the beginning?" Brady said. "So I understand? How did you meet him?"

"I was teaching in those days. Eight years ago. My first job. And you know how it is with your first job. Desperate to make a good impression."

So desperate you ignore common sense and give someone your phone number...

"So you volunteer for everything. And the school had this partnership with local businesses. Gary Cooke came in to talk to the sixth formers. Local boy made good. And then he talked to me afterwards..."

"You didn't... I don't know how to phrase it. You didn't suspect anything? There was no sign of what he was like?"

"What he was like? What *wasn't* he like? He was good looking, he was full of energy, he was funny. And he was different. He hadn't been to university. He'd left school at 16. Worked, started a business in a railway arch with his brother. By the time I met him he employed twenty, maybe twenty-five people. Selling cars. He was buying this repair shop. He was just different to all the boyfriends I'd had before."

"So you got married?"

She nodded. "St Martin's Church. June 22nd, 1991. And Sophie was born in 1994."

"And you'd left teaching by then?"

"Yes. Two years of staffroom politics was enough for me. And a friend from university had started a recruitment business. So I jumped ship and joined her. And then the wheels fell off," she said.

"What happened?"

"Like I said. I woke up one morning covered in bruises. Then my friend was ill – she had to sell the business. The new owners called me in. 'We can't understand why you need to work from home so much.' And by then I'd got Sophie..."

"So you're financially dependent on Gary?"

Sarah Cooke nodded. "For now. He owns the house. The solicitors are still arguing about the financial settlement. Shares in his business. Investments. The house. And while they're arguing he comes round and puts a spade through the car window."

Brady knew the answer to his next question before he asked it. "So when you told people about it before... What happened?"

"Someone like Bulman made a note. But you know what he's thinking. She's over-reacting. Wants attention. She needs to put a short skirt on. Make sure he gets enough sex."

Brady's coffee had gone cold. "You want another one? I've told my girlfriend to meet me here so I'm OK for time."

Sarah shook her head. "No. Thank you, but no. I need

to go to the supermarket. My daughter has become addicted to Cheerios."

She looked across the table at him. Held his eyes. "This isn't going to end well for me. I don't know how I escape it. The unpredictability. Uncertainty. Never knowing when he'll turn up next. What do I do? Move to Devon? Tell my mother she'll only see her grandchild once a year? Say goodbye to my friends? Besides, how far is Devon? Three hundred miles? He could set off first thing and be banging on my door at lunchtime."

"Why don't you get a court order? Some sort of protection?"

Sarah shook her head. "Have you any idea what a slog that is? How much it costs in time and money? How many Stan Bulman's you come across? People who simply don't believe you? And then you find your husband – ex-husband – has hired the most expensive solicitor in town. Miller bloody Stafford – that's who he used for the divorce."

That's Grace's father's firm. Not George though. Someone lower down the pecking order. Even so...

"And you stand in court and you think, 'How did this happen? I want to be safe. I want a home for my daughter. And they're putting *me* on trial.'"

"What do you want me to do?" Brady said.

Sarah Cooke shook her head. "What you've done. Listen. So that five, ten years from now, when someone comes to you and says, 'She claims he trapped her head in the car door, but I don't believe her...' Maybe you *will* believe her. It's too late for me. It's about the ones that come after me."

Dad took Mum a cup of tea every morning. Sometimes they had an argument but half an hour later they'd forgotten it. All my friends' families were the same. Or I thought they were...

"That sounds..."

"Resigned? Fatalistic? I told you. I've made a will."

Brady looked up. Saw Grace walking towards them.

"Can I phone you?"

"You mean if it happens again? You should phone 999."

"And get Bulman knocking on my door? Who'll tell me Gary's had a hard day at work? That I should make him Shepherd's Pie and give him a blow job?"

Don't say 'yes.' But what else can you say?

"OK, then. But... I'm not always on duty."

Sarah Cooke laughed. "You? You'll always be on duty, Mr Brady. That's who you are. A blind man could see that."

She stood up. Winced. Held her hand out. "Time for me to go," she said. "Your girlfriend is here."

Brady shook her hand. "Call me then," he said. "If you're frightened. Day or night. I'll do what I can."

Sarah turned. Smiled at Grace. "You've got a good one there," she said. "Don't lose him."

Grace kissed him. "Should I be suspicious, Michael Brady? Meeting other women in broad daylight? If only I knew a detective... I could get him to check up on you."

Brady smiled at her. "Why don't you do it yourself? But you'd need to keep me under close surveillance. *Very close...*"

She kissed him again. "Not in the coffee shop, Detective Constable. Go and buy me some lunch. I've booked a table at Giovanni's for tonight. Then maybe we'll see about some close surveillance..."

Assuming Sarah Cooke doesn't phone me...

6

"What's the matter?"

"I can't sleep."

"I can tell. You're talking to me. Why not?"

"No reason. It'll keep until morning. I don't want to keep you awake."

Grace leaned over and kissed him. "I am awake. Now tell me what's wrong."

"Do you want a cup of tea?"

"No. I want you to talk to me. Tell me why Sarah Cooke is keeping you awake."

"Am I that easy to read?"

"Yes. Even when you're asleep."

Michael Brady pulled her closer to him. Her head was resting on his chest. Her left arm across him. "There weren't any bruises," he said. "She wasn't obviously in pain."

"Except she winced when she stood up."

"You saw that as well? It wasn't that though. It was – I

don't even want to put it into words – it was her resignation. Her acceptance that it was going to keep happening. That we weren't interested in doing anything about it."

"Bulman, you mean?" Grace said into his chest.

"Bulman. Anyone that takes over the case. The whole system. Like it was all stacked against her."

"And what are you going to do about it?"

"What can I do, Gracie? Like Bulman said, all I'm doing is playing detective. If I say anything – make any suggestions – the whole bloody station is going to fall about laughing."

"And what happens if you *don't* say anything?"

"What do you mean?"

"What I say. What happens if you *don't* say anything?"

"Then nothing changes."

"So there's your answer."

Brady stared at the ceiling. Pulled her closer to him. "There's something else as well," he said.

"What's that?"

"Something Bulman said to me. Don't make it personal."

'Don't make it personal. You let it get personal, you take it home with you. It fucks up your marriage. And your judgement.'

"But... I can't help it, Gracie. It *is* personal. And all I've done is have coffee with her. What am I going to do in ten years' time? When people are calling *me* 'boss?' When I have to deal with a murdered child? Supposing she's the same age as one of our children? Then what?"

"You're going to deal with it. Cross one bridge at a

time. And I'll be here. I'll always be here. You need me, Michael Brady. If only to tell you what you already know. Now stop worrying, give me a kiss and go to sleep."

7

"We should have watched it at the cinema," Brady said.

"I told you that. Why didn't we?"

"Exams? One of us had 'flu? I can't remember…"

The credits rolled on *Titanic.*

Brady was on the sofa, Grace – faded jeans, old rugby shirt, hair pulled back in a ponytail – was sitting on the floor between his legs. He leaned forward and kissed the top of her head. Placed his hand lightly under her chin. Tilted her head back. "Bedtime," he said. "Unless, Miss Miller, you want to go outside and re-create the scene in the back of the car…"

She half-turned. Playfully punched him on the knee. "It's raining. It's freezing cold. I've got a report to finish in the morning. And it's Saturday night: Joe next door will be coming back from the pub."

"That's a no then?"

"It's – "

Brady's mobile rang. "Who's that at this time of night?" He looked down at his phone.

I should recognise that number...

Saw the time. 11:13.

Knew afterwards that he'd remember 11:13 for the rest of his life.

"He's here," Sarah Cooke said.

She was frightened. Terrified. Beyond terrified.

"He's here. Outside. Across the street. Please come. *Please.*"

"Mike? What is it?"

Brady ignored Grace's question. "Have you phoned 999?"

"No. I phoned you first. Like you said. Please. He's here. Across the road."

"Do it," Brady said. "Phone – "

No. She's terrified. Not thinking clearly.

"Where's your daughter?" Brady said.

"With my mum. He knows that. Every other weekend – "

"Alright. I'm coming. Lock the doors. Ten minutes."

"Mike, what on earth are you doing?"

"I'm going out, Grace. It's Sarah Cooke. Twenty-three Edgeley Road. Phone 999 for me. Give them the address. Just be calm, rational. Like you always are."

Grace stood up. "Like you're *not* being, Mike..."

'Don't make it personal.'

Too late, Stan. It already is...

BRADY PARKED THE CAR.

Not outside the house. Supposing he's looking out of the window? But not too far. Don't waste time...

He walked diagonally across the road. The orange glow of the streetlights muted by fog. Still raining, the wet tarmac glistening...

Brady looked at the house. Lights on at the front. The lounge, maybe one of the bedrooms. A normal house in a normal street. The people inside getting ready for bed...

No-one getting into a car. No-one accelerating off into the night.

A lonely dogwalker with an overweight bulldog on the other side of the road.

No-one else about – except a rookie detective standing under a streetlight.

Brady stepped back as a taxi sprayed water from a pothole. Glanced down at the road. Saw the water running down the drain.

Like your career. Still, you were a detective for ten days...

Knew he had to make a decision. Knew he was only fooling himself. He'd already made the decision.

He walked across the road. Onto the drive. Past Sarah Cooke's car. Couldn't see any movement in the house. No sound coming from it. Another car hissed past on the wet road.

You can wait. Wait for a patrol car. Say you just got here. Once you go inside... Gary Cooke could be waiting. You could contaminate the crime scene. 'And in between the crime being committed and your officers arriving, one of your team – who mistakenly thought he was a real detective – wandered round the house, Detective Chief Inspector?'

Bulman had been right. 'Defence lawyers are going to love you.'

The front door was open. Brady looked down, saw the doormat. Saw the word stencilled on it.

Welcome.

He stood under the porch. Wiped his feet. Pulled a pair of disposable gloves out of his pocket. Put his right foot on the doorstep. Leaned forward. Pushed the centre of the door. Heard Simon and Garfunkel: *Bridge over Troubled Water.*

Could never listen to the song again.

Light from the lounge spilled out into the hall.

You can't hear any sirens. No flashing lights outside. There's still time to leave...

"Sarah? It's Michael Brady." He was competing with Paul and Art. *America* now.

"Sarah?"

He stood still. Listened for movement.

What if there's someone else in the house?

There wasn't. He knew it. Some instinct. Just him and Sarah. Just the two of them.

Michael Brady glanced at his right hand.

Yes, you're still wearing gloves. As if they've fallen off somehow...

Pushed the lounge door slightly.

Stepped inside.

Saw Sarah Cooke.

Blue jeans, dark blue sweatshirt. Bare feet.

Swap the sweatshirt for an old rugby shirt and... And she's dressed exactly like Grace. The same colour hair...

A night in. Watching a movie. There was a bottle of red wine on the coffee table. The glass had fallen on the floor. Next to Sarah Cooke's right foot.

Red wine, maroon carpet. At least it won't stain...

She was half on the floor, half on the sofa. Her body twisted, her face resting on a cushion.

Like Grace. When she turned to punch me. Or if I hadn't been there. If she'd suddenly felt tired. Twisted round and put her head on the cushion for five minutes.

Is that how she died? Did he suffocate her? She'd have struggled more. Kicked out. Kicked the wine bottle off the table...

There's no blood. Did he strangle her?

Brady fought the temptation to bend down. Move her hair to one side. Look for the bruises on her neck.

Fought it.

Lost.

Yes. There. Two red lines. Maybe two inches long. Forefinger, middle finger. There'll be the mark from his thumb on the other side.

Had enough sense not to move the body to look for it.

'He's here. Outside. Across the street. Please...'

Too late. Gary Cooke was here. Now he's gone.

8

Michael Brady looked down at the body.

I had coffee with her. Four days ago...

Let his eyes wander from her neck. Across her shoulder. Down her arm, past her elbow. Her forearm. Down to her wrist, her hand. The hand that was clutching a picture. A four year old girl in a long white dress. Angel's wings and a tinsel crown. The Angel Gabriel.

The Christmas tree lights were twinkling. A home-made fairy on top of the tree. Paul and Art had left *America. El Condor Pasa...*

Brady looked back at the body.

Is this my fault? Was there something I missed when she told me the story? Something I should have done differently when she phoned?

"I'm sorry, Sarah," he said out loud. "This... I've let you down. I... I'll find who did this. Gary. We'll find him. He can't be far away."

He pressed his fingers to his lips. Bent forward.

Touched them to Sarah Cooke's cheek. "I'm sorry," he said again. "I promise..."

Brady saw something out of the corner of his eye. Flashing lights reflecting on the window. Heard the siren. Walked into the hall. Out of the front door. Down the drive. Saw the police car come to a stop. Two men in uniform. Remembered to pull his gloves off. Stuffed them in his pocket.

Eddie Harvey. Brady had been on patrol with him a few times. And Dave Elleray.

"Mike? What the hell are you doing here?"

"She phoned me. I saw her the other day. With Stan Bulman. She had my number."

Harvey looked at him. "That's a bit bloody odd. You're not on duty? So who phoned 999?"

"My girlfriend phoned. And no, I'm not. I was just about to go in."

Harvey shook his head, "Don't. Not if you're not on duty. Stay here. Take these – " Harvey passed him some keys. "Sit in the car. Out of the rain. Let us take a look."

Brady opened the passenger door of the white Rover. Slid inside. Realised how wet he was. Realised he'd have some explaining to do.

Can I say I went inside the house? Saw the body? No. Not in a thousand years. Supposing Fitzpatrick asks me? He'll know if I'm lying...

Five minutes. Ten minutes. Harvey was walking down the drive. Brady opened the car door. "She's dead," he said simply. "Judging by the marks on her neck, strangled. When did she phone you?"

"Just after eleven," Brady said. "Eleven-thirteen."

There's no point saying anything else. It'll be on the phone bill.

"And you've only just got here?" Harvey said. "You're not that far away are you?"

No, I'm not. I've got ten minutes to account for.

"The car wouldn't start."

Brady heard his mother. *'The more you lie, Michael, the more you will need to lie.'*

Harvey nodded. "You might as well piss off home. Get yourself dry. They're all on their way. Ambulance. Stan Bulman. SOCO. No bloody way any of us are going home before four in the morning."

"I should stay…"

Harvey shook his head. "What for, Mike? You reported it. You got here. God knows Fitzpatrick will have plenty of questions on Monday. But for now you might as well be at home in bed."

9

She was waiting for him in the hall as he came through the door. "Are you OK, Mike? What happened?"

Brady stood in the doorway. Still in his wet coat. Shook his head. Stared into space. "She's dead," he said. "He strangled her."

Grace walked towards him. Eased his coat off. Let it fall on the floor. Pulled him close. "What happened?"

"She's dead," Brady said again. "He strangled her. I saw the marks. On her neck..."

Grace took him by the hand. Led him into the lounge. "Sit down. I'll make some tea. Then you can talk. Or not talk. Whatever you want."

Brady sat on the sofa.

All I ever wanted to do. Be a detective. And this is it. A dead body in the middle of the night. A woman who smiled at me. Frightened but alive. Thinking about her daughter.

How many more times will she need to make me tea?

Grace was back. She sat down. Put her hand on his cheek. Tilted his head. Forced him to look at her. "Drink your tea. Sit with me. Don't say anything if you don't want to. We'll sit here all night if it helps. Whatever we have to do. Alright?"

I love her. I'm going to marry her. I have to tell her the truth.

"I went in the house," he said.

She pulled him towards her. Cradled his head against her shoulder. "You don't have to tell me. It's fine."

Brady pulled away.

"I went in the house," he said again. "I saw the body."

"When the patrol car came?"

Brady shook his head. "Before. On my own."

"Mike, I'm confused. You told me to phone 999. I did that. There must have been a patrol car."

"There was. But... I was there first. Lights were on. I went in. Saw her."

Grace moved back. Put space between them. Looked into his eyes. "You're saying you went into the house? On your own? Not knowing what you'd find? Not knowing who might be in there?"

Brady nodded. "Yes, that's what I did. I found her. Strangled."

That's her you've-left-the-toilet-seat-up face. Times ten. Times a hundred...

"You know how – bloody hell, Mike – you know how dangerous that was? I love you, Mike. But that was just bloody stupid."

"What could I do, Grace? I swore an oath to uphold the law."

"And in six months' time you're going to swear an oath to me. Love, honour and cherish. And you can't do that if you're wandering round a house with a man that puts a spade through a car window. And strangles his wife."

"Ex-wife," Brady said. "And I know, I'm sorry."

She reached out. Took his tea off the table. Passed it to him. "Here, drink this. Don't say anything else. Drink your tea and then we'll go to bed. Let me hold you."

"I can't, Grace. Not straightaway. Let me sit down here for a minute. Let the adrenalin go out of my system. Let the stress wash away."

"You're sure?"

"I'm sure. You go to bed. You've got that report to do in the morning. I'll be up in five minutes. I promise. I love you."

"I love you too, Michael Brady. And make sure you do."

BRADY SAT ON THE SOFA. Realised his jeans were still damp. Realised he couldn't go upstairs and change because he couldn't say no to Grace a second time. Wondered if she'd known he needed to be on his own.

Stared into space. Heard the rain beating against the window. Saw Sarah Cooke.

My first murder victim. Blue jeans. Dressed like Grace.

Saw her face resting on the cushion. Watched his hand move her hair to one side. Saw the two red lines.

Forefinger, middle finger. Thumb on the other side.

Saw her arm, her hand. The hand clutching the photo of the Angel Gabriel. Heard *El Condor Pasa* over the rain...

. . .

"I WOKE UP," Grace said at four in the morning. "I needed a glass of water. I won't take 'no' for an answer. Come back to bed with me."

She held her hand out. Michael Brady did as he was told.

10

'What for, Mike? You reported it. God knows Fitzpatrick will have plenty of questions on Monday.'

Jim Fitzpatrick didn't wait that long. Brady's phone beeped at 8am on Sunday morning. He was still in bed. Not even sure if he'd slept.

My office. 11am.

"SO TELL ME WHAT HAPPENED, Michael. Slowly. Step-by-step. I'm a simple man."

"When I was there with Bulman, sir – "

"Boss, remember. And that's a good enough place to start."

"Sorry." Brady looked up at Fitzpatrick. Found the courage to look him straight in the eye. "I'm sorry, sir. I'm nervous."

Fitzpatrick nodded. "So you should be. But let's hear the story."

"When I was there with Bulman... She asked for my

number. I think... She said she wanted to tell her story –
to someone who might believe her, I suppose."

"Did that not strike you as odd. Woman who's been
abused? Wants to talk to a man? Surely she'd have asked
to speak to a woman." Fitzpatrick gestured at the next
office. "Tessa, if she wants to speak to someone."

"I said that to her, boss. She said I looked sympathetic."

Fitzpatrick raised his eyebrows. Didn't say anything.

"She rang me, I said 'yes.' I met her for coffee. I
shouldn't have. But I did."

"Alright, I'll score you one point for that. It's a good
quality for a copper to have. People thinking they can talk
to you. And it's your first case. She made you feel important. You think, 'maybe I've got what it takes.'"

Brady looked down. "Yes, boss. I guess so."

That's exactly how she made me feel.

"Did you tell anyone you were meeting her?"

"No, boss. Well... that is, Grace. My girlfriend. I told
her to meet me there for lunch."

"So you told your girlfriend, but you didn't tell Stan
Bulman."

"No, boss."

How long before I qualify as a solicitor? Three years?

"You didn't tell anyone because you thought 'unofficial' was the best way. Because you thought she'd be more
open if she was talking to a friend. Because you thought
you'd learn more that way."

Brady nodded. Felt ashamed. "Yes, boss. I thought...
Seeing as nothing was going to come of her complaint
that... It *was* unofficial."

"Summarise it for me. What did she tell you?"

"Everything. The history. How she met him. How good it was at first. How it changed. Then she was pregnant. And gradually – there's no other way to put it, boss – gradually the cage closed around her."

"When did he start hitting her?"

"From what she said... More or less as soon as they were married."

"Have you written it up? This meeting?"

"Yes, boss. Notes. On my computer."

"But you haven't shown it to anyone?"

"No, boss."

Fitzpatrick nodded. "Let me have it. No-one else. You understand?"

"Yes, boss."

"So... Saturday night... She rings you?"

"We'd just finished watching a film. She rang me – "

"What did she say? Word for word."

"He's here. Outside. Across the street. Please come."

"How did she sound?"

"Terrified. Not logical. That's why we – Grace – rang 999."

"Then what?"

"Grace made the phone call. I jumped in the car."

"And..."

"Parked. Maybe a hundred yards away. The opposite side of the street. In case he was inside. But there was nothing to see. A wet street. A few cars..."

How long can I spend describing the outside? Not long enough.

"...Sarah Cooke's car parked in the drive. No-one else in sight."

"Dog walkers?"

"One, boss. With an overweight bulldog."

Fitzpatrick nodded. "He won't be hard to find if we need him. Then what?"

Time to crawl to Grace's dad. Ah well, qualified in three years. A partner by my mid-thirties. And Grace won't find me on the sofa at four in the morning...

"Then what, Mike?"

He'll know if I'm lying...

"I went in the house."

Jim Fitzpatrick nodded. Tapped his middle finger on the desk. Nodded again. "You've just told me you parked a hundred yards away. 'In case he was inside.' But you went in the house. On your own. No back up. Every chance there's a murderer waiting for you. He's just killed someone. So he's nothing to lose by killing you. Eddie Harvey is five, ten minutes away?"

"Ten minutes, boss. Maybe less."

"And you go in there. And you see the body. Did you touch anything?"

"Nothing in the house. The doors. I pushed the middle of both doors."

"Gloves?"

"Yes, boss."

Is he going to ask me if I touched the body? Does he know I did? Is he going to let me get away with it?

Brady's mouth was dry.

If I was a suspect I could ask for a drink of water...

"How did you feel?"

"How did I feel?" Brady repeated, caught completely off guard by the question.

Fitzpatrick nodded. "You know me by now. Ask the question they don't expect. How did you feel? You've interviewed her with Bulman. She told you her story. You've bought her coffee. Now she's dead. You're standing over the body. So how did you feel?"

"I felt..."

How the hell did I feel? And can I say it out loud?

"I felt responsible, boss. Like it was my fault in some way. And... I don't like to say this..."

"Try me."

"'Excited' is the wrong word. I felt like I was in the right place, if that makes sense. That... I was where I was supposed to be."

"That you were doing what God put you on this Earth to do?"

"Yes, boss. Exactly that."

Fitzpatrick nodded. "It was the same for me. Just outside Bolton. One of those clear, crisp autumn mornings. A hint of the first frost. A clearing in a wood. A shallow grave. She was sixteen years old." He paused. "We caught him. My boss gave me some advice. I've never forgotten it. 'You want to catch a killer?' he said. 'You've got to think like a killer. You've got to *be* the killer. And the victim. You've got to get inside their heads.' I can hear him now."

Fitzpatrick swivelled in his chair. Looked out of the window. Left Brady hanging for ten seconds. Turned back to him.

"One last question. Did you tell your girlfriend that

you went in the house?"

Brady nodded. "Yes, boss. I think now... Maybe I shouldn't have done."

"Because she'll worry. Right. It's a bloody tough job being married to a copper. You'll learn there are things it's best not to tell her. And she'll learn there are things it's best not to ask. Because when you've finished thinking like a killer – when you finished killing, or being killed – you've got to go round Tesco with her."

"I'm beginning to realise that..."

"OK. Marriage guidance over. I'm going to say two things to you. One. You were stupid last night. Beyond stupid. And I don't like stupid coppers on my team. You could have fucked the investigation before it had started. You understand that?"

"Yes, boss,"

"Good. I give everyone that works for me a 'Get-out-of-Jail' card. They can use it once. One fuck-up. People have been calling me 'boss' for 15 years now. No-one's ever used it as fast as you have, Mike."

Brady nodded. Knew he didn't need to speak.

"The second thing. A police station, a murder enquiry. It's like a football team. It's not just your skill on the pitch. It's the dressing room as well. Can you survive the bullies? The old pros who want you to fail? And trust me, Mike, you're a graduate. Not everyone's impressed. There'll be plenty out there that *do* want you to fail. So going into the house – and the report – they stay between you and me. Therefore, *Acting* Detective Constable Brady, let me ask you again, for the record. Did you go into the house?"

Brady looked across the desk. Seized the lifeline he'd just been thrown. Swore a lifelong oath of allegiance to Jim Fitzpatrick. "No, boss."

"Wise decision."

Fitzpatrick looked across the desk at him. "You're a bright lad, Mike. You'll do well. But don't go into a house without back-up again. When are you getting married?"

This time Brady was ready for him. "June 12th, boss."

"Right. Grace, did you say?"

"Yes, boss."

"Grace doesn't want me standing on her doorstep. Seeing my face. Knowing what's happened. Think on that, Michael... Now bugger off and do door-to-door with Stan Bulman."

"On a Sunday, boss?"

"There's been a murder, Mike. Apologise and crack on. Let's get this one wrapped up. And remember what I've said to you."

11

"Door to door," Bulman said. "I hate door to door. It's either winter and you're freezing your bollocks off, or it's summer and you're dripping sweat. And no bastard offers you a cuppa. Which side of the road do you want?"

"It's winter," Brady said. "But the sun's on this side of the street. So you have Sarah's side and I'll cross over and do the other side. See if the sun compensates you for January."

"Bloody hell," Bulman said. "You might have a future in the police force after all."

A TEXTBOOK CASE, Brady thought afterwards. Absolutely textbook. Clean, simple, a reliable witness. Every young detective's dream.

"Good morning. I'm sorry to disturb you. My name's Michael Brady. I'm with Greater Manchester Police. We're making enquiries – "

"I saw, young man. Last night. I was looking out of the window. Just on the off-chance, obviously."

A retired schoolteacher. Maybe she'd been a librarian. Miss Marple's twin sister.

"I saw him going in."

"You saw who going in, Mrs..."

"Miss. Jefferson. I saw the – is he the husband? The one who's always round there. Big. Hunched. An aggressive way of walking. He went back to his car. Twice, I think. Slammed the door every time. Woke the dead I shouldn't wonder."

"You saw his car?"

"How could I not see it? Parked right outside my house. One of those foreign sports cars. Why people don't buy British I shall never know."

"And have you any idea what time this was, Miss Jefferson?"

"I'd just finished watching an Agatha Christie – *Death on the Nile*, have you seen it? Very good – so just after eleven."

"And you're sure you saw him going into the house?"

"Absolutely. She opened the door."

"Do you know what time he left?"

"Ah, there I can't help you, young man. I went to bed. I'm not one of these neighbours who spies on people, you know..."

So you didn't see a stupid young copper going into the house? Thank you, God.

"...And then obviously the noise of the sirens woke me up. Comings and goings all night. And that poor girl lying there all the time. Just make sure you catch him, officer."

"Irene Jefferson," Brady said. "Retired English teacher. Saw a big man with an 'aggressive' walk going into the house just after eleven. And he had 'a foreign sports car.'"

"A red Porsche," Bulman said. "That's what Gary Cooke was driving last time I saw him. That's good enough for me. And not too late for a bacon sandwich in the canteen. Top work, young Padawan. Buy you a bacon butty I shall."

"Don't you think... Don't you think it's a bit *too* good to be true? Late at night. It's raining. Traffic on the road..."

"Who are you? Perry bloody Mason? Defence lawyer? Don't look a gift horse in the mouth."

"I thought you said Gary Cooke was a good lad?"

"Yeah well. Maybe she provoked him."

"Did you ever pull wings off butterflies?" Brady said.

Grace looked up. Narrowed her eyes. "I'm not sure I want to marry a man who asks me a question like that. But I assume this is leading somewhere?"

"Yes, it is. It's accepted wisdom, isn't it? Murderers start off by pulling wings off butterflies – "

"Or finding the person they live with has left the toilet seat up again."

"Oh. Sorry. Hear me out before you reach for the carving knife. There was a boy when I was growing up. I'd see him walking his dog. Always yanking the lead.

Nearly pulling the dog off its feet. I could never understand why his parents let him take the dog out."

"Maybe they were the same?"

"Maybe... Are you leaving those chips?"

Grace sighed and pushed the plate across the table. "When's your next police medical, darling?"

"What I'm saying is – apart from we need to go to Whitby for some *real* fish and chips – is I *do* see the link between a kid mistreating animals and turning into a psychopath. But I don't see the link between persistent abuse and murder."

"I don't follow you."

"Because if Sarah Cooke was the butterfly, and Gary was the kid pulling her wings off, that's what he enjoyed. I don't see why he'd kill the butterfly."

"Maybe he lost his temper? If he puts a spade through her car window what else is he capable of? And that's not a spur of the moment thing, Mike. That's serious anger. He's got to walk to the garage. Maybe break a padlock. Find the spade..."

"You're probably right. And all the evidence points that way. I just wish I knew more about it. I'm beginning to think I should have done psychology, not law." He stood up, reached across the table for Grace's plate and started to walk towards the kitchen.

"What happened to him?" Grace said.

"Who?"

"The boy that was cruel to his dog. The one that proves your theory."

Brady laughed. "I don't know. His dad got put in prison. The family moved away."

12

"Everyone here?"

Michael Brady sat at the back of the room.

My first case conference. Or team meeting? I don't even know what it's called...

Jim Fitzpatrick at the front. Half a dozen detectives in various stages of age, experience and casual dress. Eddie Harvey and Dave Elleray to report on what they found. DS Tess Knightly – late-30s, unmarried, the subject of plenty of suggestions behind her back and none at all to her face – sat to one side. The door opened. Stan Bulman – firmly attached to another Marlboro – mumbled an apology and sat down.

"Right," Fitzpatrick said. "Sarah Cooke, murdered on Saturday night. Cause of death, strangulation. Time of death... We know she was alive at 11:13. We know she was dead when Eddie and Dave arrived at 11:42. So a twenty-nine minute window, gentlemen. And lady. Sorry, Tess."

Not a twenty-nine minute window. A ten minute window.

Fifteen at the most. Between the phone call and me parking the car.

"Why 11:13, boss?" Bulman asked.

"Because that's when she made the phone call, Stan."

"999?"

"No."

He's given me twelve extra minutes. But he's not going to lie.

"She phoned Mike Brady."

Everyone turned to look at him. "Why?" was the politest comment he heard.

"Mike? You want to tell the story?"

Brady nodded. Wondered if he was supposed to stand up. Decided against it. Felt his mouth go dry.

'Can you survive the bullies? The old pros who want you to fail? And trust me, Mike, you're a graduate. Not everyone's impressed. There'll be plenty out there that do want you to fail.'

I'm going to give them plenty of ammunition...

"She asked for my number. When I saw her with Stan. Then we had coffee. She said she wanted to tell someone her story. She phoned me on Saturday night. I went round to the house. Got there at the same time as Eddie and Dave."

Bulman was shaking his head. Bill Slater – a few weeks from retiring – was next to him, gazing up to Heaven. Brady could feel it. Equal parts of scepticism, hostility – and astonishment that anyone so stupid could get through the selection process.

"What did she say?" Slater asked. "Not when you

were swapping cake recipes over coffee. When it got serious."

"She said, 'He's here. Outside. Across the street.'"

Fitzpatrick took over. "What did you say?"

"I asked if her child was there."

"You didn't ask 'who?' Or what was he doing across the street?"

"No, boss. Because her tone of voice... She was terrified. I assumed it was Gary. The most important thing seemed to be... Well, to get round there."

Two people started to speak. Fitzpatrick held his hand up. "There's no need for any comments. I've already discussed it with Brady. All we need to take from that is she was alive at 11:13. Eddie, your turn."

Harvey – awkwardly self-conscious in his uniform – did stand up. "Like you said, sir, we got there at 11:42. The front door was open. Lights on in the lounge. She was half on the floor, half on the sofa. Very clearly dead."

"Signs of a struggle?"

Harvey shook his head. "Not really, sir. There was a wine glass on the floor. But nothing else. Wine bottle still on the table. Christmas tree in the corner. Christmas cards. Everything you'd expect."

"Seems a bit late, boss," Bill Slater said. "Christmas decorations still up on January 9th."

Fitzpatrick shrugged. "Probably kept them up until her daughter went back to school. Maybe she was waiting for the little girl to come back. Put the tree up together, take it down together."

"You can all see the photos," he said, gesturing behind him. "They all confirm what Eddie has said." Fitzpatrick reached forward, picked a piece of A4 off his desk. "The report from our colleague the Grim Reaper. Very clearly death by strangulation. Hyoid bone broken. Marks visible on the neck – "

Two red lines. Maybe two inches long. Forefinger, middle finger. There'll be the mark from his thumb on the other side.

Brady didn't need to hear the autopsy report.

" – And marks on the back of her neck as well. The learned Dr Kearney thinks – but is at pains to stress it is only supposition – that he held her with his left hand and strangled her with his right."

"You mean he was holding her?" Tess said. "Then he moved his right hand to her neck and started squeezing? Need to be a bloody strong bloke to do that."

"That's what Kearney's suggesting," Fitzpatrick said.

"He's saying Gary Cooke did it," Bulman said flatly.

"Let's not jump to conclusions. But you're probably right, Stan. Almost certainly right." He turned back to Brady. "Eye witness from the house to house, Mike?"

This time Brady did stand up. "Irene Jefferson, boss. Retired English teacher. Lives across the road. Saw a big man with what she described as an 'aggressive' walk going into the house just after eleven. Described the car as a 'foreign sports car.' Said he slammed the car door two or three times."

"Which suggests someone in a temper. OK," Fitzpatrick said. "I want to take this one gently. I'll bring Gary Cooke in this afternoon. No doubt with a very expensive solicitor. I'm not arresting him at this stage – I'm waiting for fingerprints and DNA. But right now we're not looking for anyone else. One more thing – " Fitzpatrick held his hand up as everyone started to leave. "Some of you know Gary Cooke. Football, socially, you might have taken your cars in there. Not a word of this gets out. Understood?"

There was a general murmur of assent. The meeting started to break up.

Don't say anything. All you can do is look stupid. Don't –

"Boss?"

"What is it, Mike? And all of you, if someone's got something to say, sit down and listen."

Bulman was reaching for another Marlboro. Bill Slater was contemplating Heaven again.

"Boss, no-one's saying Gary Cooke was a saint. He clearly abused her. He was controlling her. But does that make him a murderer? Is it... I don't know. An automatic progression?"

Several people laughed. "He put a shovel through her car window," Bulman said. "He had a temper. Like I said, she probably provoked him."

"You're missing the point. Do you not think he might have *needed* her in some way? Doing what he did... It must have given him some pleasure. Why kill her? Do you not think – "

"For God's sake. He's replaced her with a Page 3 girl. Course he didn't need her."

"She was – " But Brady knew he'd lost. The meeting was over. It was lunchtime. The canteen was calling.

"Never make a bloody copper in a million years." Bill Slater said it just loud enough to make sure he heard.

Maybe he's right...

13

"You think Fitz hung you out to dry?"

"No, I think he was testing me. Some sort of initiation ceremony, maybe."

"Baptism of fire? Anyway, we're here," Tess said.

The meeting had finished. Brady's choice had been simple. Brave the rain on the way to the sandwich shop – or brave the sarcasm in the canteen.

Then Tess Knightly had taken charge. "Get your coat, young man. We've got an hour."

"Where are we going?"

"You'll see."

"Can I ask another question?" Brady said.

"Of course."

"What do I call you?"

Tess laughed. "Thanks for asking. Not 'sarge.' That's for Ernie Moss. Men that are going bald and letting their belts out. Skip, if you want a title. Or Tess, which is perfectly fine."

Brady followed her down to the car park. Ten minutes

later they pulled up outside a double-fronted Victorian house. The bottom half of one window was boarded up. SHIS was stencilled on the glass above it.

"SHIS?" Brady said.

"Support and Hope in Stretford. They decided against Support and Hope in Trafford. I can't for the life of me work out why. I help out one afternoon a week. It's a women's refuge. Well, it's the offices. Clearly I can't take a man into a women's refuge."

Tess parked the car. Led Brady through a hall that was an equal mix of ads and mailboxes for a dozen different organisations.

She knocked lightly on a door and opened it.

"Angie? I'd like you to meet Michael Brady. Acting Detective Constable Michael Brady. He might just be one of the good guys."

"A good guy? Rides into work on a silver unicorn does he?" Angie – mid 30s, wild red hair, denim dungarees with two white paint splashes – held her hand out. "Sorry. The natural cynicism of early middle age. If Tess says you're a good guy that's a decent reference. What can I do for you?"

"We're working on a case," Tess said.

"The girl in Stockport?"

Tess raised her eyebrows. "Did I say that, Ange? But there's a background of domestic abuse. And... some home truths would be useful. Our young friend had the balls to question the accepted wisdom in a roomful of coppers this morning. I thought I'd strike while the iron's hot."

"You want coffee?" Angie said. "Sorry, I don't hold out much hope on biscuits."

Tess shook her head. "We've not got that long. Give him some background. Let him ask a few questions."

Angie gestured at a battered sofa. "Sit down. Background... There's been a thousand women through our front door. And a thousand different stories. Every case is different. The official figures say one woman in ten might be a victim. You want my opinion? It's closer to one in five. And if you think it's only working class women whose husbands are out of work, think again. It's like child abuse. Incest. A lot of the victims don't come forward. They're ashamed. Think it's their fault. Do their best to hide it. And the scars don't always show."

"Why?" Brady said. "What triggers it? I've got a girlfriend. I couldn't even think..."

"What triggers it? What *doesn't* trigger it? Drugs, alcohol, losing their job, keeping their job. Stress. Boredom."

"Are some men just... I don't know. Programmed to do it? Pre-disposed?"

"If you went to the refuge and talked to some of the girls they'd say *all* men. Me? I don't think so. But it's bloody difficult to argue with someone who's sitting on our sofa and telling you this boyfriend doesn't hit her quite as hard as the last one."

Angie took a weary breath. "But domestic abuse isn't about hitting someone. It's about control. Power over someone else. It's about hiding your own inadequacies. Sometimes it's about anger at being dependent on the woman you've just punched."

"Dependent?" Brady said. "You mean he needs her in some way?"

"Co-dependency if you want the technical term. She needs him. Money, somewhere to live maybe. And in his own fucked-up way – yes, he needs her."

"Does it escalate?" Brady said.

I don't like asking the questions. Maybe this is Tess's version of the initiation ceremony...

"If he hits her three times this week does he hit her four times next week?"

"Yes, sometimes," Angie said. "And hopefully something snaps and she comes knocking on our door. 'It's getting worse. He's going to kill me.' If I had a pound for every time I've heard that – " Angie gestured at the paint splashes " – some other daft bugger would be painting the ceiling."

'I'm thirty years old and I've made a will. Before he does me some serious damage. How many women of my age make a will?'

"How often does it lead to murder?" Brady said.

Angie shook her head. "You can't say. Obviously if a man's been violent before there's an increased risk of murder. But even then it's not absolute. Some men tick all the boxes. Some don't tick any. There have been 70 year old men. Never been violent in their lives. The wife asks for a divorce, something snaps."

"Is that a trigger? Moving out? Wanting a divorce?"

"Yes. How are you doing for time, Tess? You know I can talk about this all day. Especially when someone's paying attention."

"We're good," Tess said. "Ten minutes or so."

"Yes, then," Angie said. "They're losing control. They don't like that. So very often the violence escalates. Especially if there's another man involved. Whether he's real or imagined."

"If I can't have her no-one else can?"

Angie nodded. "Yep, pretty much."

Brady looked at Tess. Made an 'am I alright to ask this?' gesture. She nodded.

"We're speaking in confidence here?"

Angie laughed. "In confidence? There's your doctor. Your solicitor. There's the confessional. And then there are the stories I hear. And can't get out of my head at three in the morning."

So I'm not the only one sitting on the sofa in the middle of the night...

She nodded. "Yes, we're speaking in confidence."

"Is there... Are there any signs? You know, people say kids who torture animals..."

"Right. And there are just as many serial killers who loved their pets. Have you heard of Blondi?"

Brady shook his head.

"Hitler's dog. Spent a lot of his final hours taking her for walks outside the bunker. She slept by his bed. But you want a sign? I'll give you a sign. Strangulation."

"Strangulation?"

"Yes. Not fatal. It's a criminal offence in some countries. Here? Our politicians can't be arsed. But someone did a study. I'll find it for you. If someone's strangled by a partner they're seven times more likely to be murdered by the same partner."

'Pass me your coat, I'll hang it up for you.'

'Thank you.'

'Scarf?'

'It's not that warm in here. I'll keep it on.'

"So if someone keeps their scarf on..." Brady said.

Angie nodded. "A woman walks in here with a scarf on – assuming it's not freezing cold – and I know what I'm going to see. It's a serious warning sign. And it sounds like you'd better read the autopsy report, Tess. Evidence of prior bruising."

Tess stood up. "That's this afternoon taken care of, Ange. And thanks for being gentle with him."

Brady held his hand out. "Thank you, I appreciate it."

"You're welcome. And here," Angie said, handing him a business card. "Find a way to pay me back some time. But remember what I said, Michael. Each case is different. Don't rely on the conventional wisdom. And don't spend all your time looking for demons in the past. If you do that you're going to miss a hell of a lot of demons in the present."

"She never went there then," Brady said as they got back into the car.

"Sarah? Not to my knowledge. Chances are I'd have come across her."

"Do you think he did it, skip?"

"Gary Cooke?" Tess replied. "No, I don't think he did it. I know he did it."

14

"Can you stand up a minute?"

"Why?"

"I need to act out a murder. I'm sorry, I need to strangle you."

"I'd rather have a cup of tea..."

"Let me explain."

"You won't get a lighter sentence, Mike. The judge won't be swayed by 'he explained why he was strangling her...'"

"I'll just have to rely on my good looks and charm to influence the jury then. Let me be serious for a minute."

Brady shuffled across the settee so he could turn and face her. The settee they'd bought at the weekend – which Brady had finally, grudgingly admitted was bigger/comfier/a lot more modern than 'that settee from your old flat.'

"I went to a women's refuge today," he said. "The office. Tess Knightly took me."

Grace started to make a joke. "No, don't," Brady said.

"It was... I don't know. Moving in a way. I talked to the woman who runs it. She gave me some background."

"About Sarah Cooke? What did she say?"

How much of this can I tell her? How much should I tell her?

Brady nodded. "Turns out I was wrong."

Grace opened her eyes wide. Raised her eyebrows in mock-surprise. "No, darling. You're a man, that's not possible."

"Sadly it is. Turns out you don't need to pull the wings off butterflies. Hitler loved his dog. Took her for walks outside the bunker."

"What else?"

"Far more women are abused than most people believe – "

"Most *men* believe..."

"That it's about control, not punching someone. That it can lead to murder. That it escalates if they want a divorce or move away. And that every case is different. I shouldn't rely on conventional wisdom. There was something else as well..."

"What's that?"

"From the case conference. Stand up."

"I'm not sure about this, Michael Brady. First you ask me if I pull the wings off butterflies. Now you want to strangle me?"

"Sorry..."

Grace slowly got to her feet. Brady moved towards her. Put his left arm round her. Pulled her to him. Brought his right hand up to her cheek. Traced his nails slowly over her cheek. Murmured, "You're beautiful..."

Moved his hand lower. Let it rest on her neck. Spread his fingers.

Grace looked into his eyes. Held them. "You know some women like this don't you?"

Brady bent his head. Kissed her. "We're working."

She kissed him back. Let her hand fall. Moved it over his jeans. "That's not what it feels like…"

Brady stepped away from her. "You could do it," he said. "Put your arms round someone. One hand on their throat. One hand behind their head."

"But she'd fight."

"Yes. So he'd need to be bigger, stronger. And determined to kill her."

Grace turned her back. Stepped away from him. Crossed her hands. Pulled the rugby shirt over her head. "What else did you learn? Apart from something new about your soon-to-be-wife?"

Brady watched her unhook the black bra. Saw it fall to the floor. "Every case is different," he said. Saw Grace unzip her jeans. Start to inch them over her hips. "And that if I chase demons in the past – Christ, Grace – I'll miss demons in the present."

"No time like the present," Grace whispered, and turned to face him.

15

"Mike?"

"Yes, boss?"

"I've got a job for you. I want you to go and interview someone."

"With Stan Bulman?"

"No. On your own. Stan's having his annual medical. Tess Knightly's in a policy meeting with me. Two people are off sick. So it's just you and Darren Gilman."

"I don't want to sound stupid, boss, but who's Darren Gilman?"

"Gary Cooke's brother. Half-brother."

Half-brother? Sarah didn't say. But why would she?

Fitzpatrick nodded. "You know they started the business together?"

"Yes. That's something I do know."

"Right. Go and get some background. I'm dotting the i's and crossing the t's. I've spoken to Cooke – and his very sharp solicitor. Total waste of time. So let's get as much background as we can while I wait for everything to come

back from the lab. Just go through the details. Here – "
Fitzpatrick handed him a piece of paper. "Here's the
address. Eleven o'clock. He knows you're coming."

"You guys usually go round in pairs don't you? Like
teenage girls?"

Brady decided the best response was to laugh. "Usually. But we're short-staffed. So here I am. One copper,
one notebook."

Darren Gilman looked out of place. Far too big for the
house. Almost completely bald, a goatee beard with his
top lip shaved. Crooked teeth. A dark green sweatshirt,
navy tracksuit bottoms, bare feet and flip-flops.

He nodded. Showed Brady into the lounge. "Your
boss said you needed some background."

Brady looked round the room. There wasn't much
doubt which brother was making the money. 'Gary's
moved out to Cheshire,' Bulman had told him. 'Village
full of solicitors, footballers and wide boys.'

His half-brother – Brady guessed he was around 40 –
was in a neglected semi in Ashton-under-Lyne. A hopeful
'For Sale' sign outside. And a lounge with all the furniture shoehorned into one half of the room.

"This won't take long, Mr Gilman. Just a few
questions."

"Like I said. Fire away." He rested his left foot on his
right knee. His second toe was much longer than his big
toe, Brady noticed.

*That probably means something. Surprised it wasn't part
of the training course...*

"Gary's business? You started it together."

He nodded. "Gilman and Cooke. Gary Cooke Cars now. Obviously."

"Buying and selling cars?"

"Top end cars. Gary always knew where he was going. He was never going to fart around with Ford Fiestas. First car we bought was a Stag. Triumph Stag. Bought it off a widow. Been left outside for three years. Gary restored it. Beautiful. We made about four grand. And we were off. He was off, I should say."

"But you were partners?"

"In name. I was working as an accountant. We were partners 'cos that was the only way Mum would lend him the money to buy the Stag. I'm eight years older. 'The sensible one.' Gary's dad... He was a bit wild. Mine worked at the town hall."

"But you ended up working together?"

"Yeah. Biggest mistake I ever made." Darren Gilman slowly stood up. "You want tea or anything?"

"No, I'm fine, thanks," Brady said. "Police canteen. One's enough for the day."

"Give me two minutes." He lumbered into the kitchen.

Brady looked around. There was a gaping hole by the lounge window, the carpet in front of it brighter and cleaner. No pictures. Not even the obligatory wedding day. A big TV, a remote control on the arm of what was clearly the only chair Gilman ever sat in.

The thinnest cat Brady had ever seen brushed against his legs. The sun was shining on Gilman's chair through the window. The cat didn't hesitate.

"Linda told me not to." He was back, a Manchester United mug looking far too small for his hand. "'You can't trust him,' she said. Hey! Piss off, you."

Gilman quickly dipped the end of his fingers in his tea. Flicked it at the cat. A screech. A flash of ginger fur. And it was gone.

"Bloody nuisance. Linda's obviously. Where was I? Gary persuaded me. The days when he could persuade me to do anything. By this time he's employing around twenty people. He needs someone to do the books. Order the parts. Pay the wages. And Linda's not very well. She's started tripping up. Falling over. Can't take the lid off the marmalade. That's when I first noticed it. One morning at breakfast. Told her she had to see the doctor. So I pack my job in. Gary tells me it'll be alright. Four days a week with him. 'The rest of the time you can look after Linda' he says."

Brady glanced at the empty half of the room.

Darren Gilman nodded. "That's where her bed was. Under the window. She liked to look outside. Watch the world go by. She made me throw bread out in the front garden. So she could watch the birds."

"Can I ask..."

"ALS. Amyotrophic Lateral Sclerosis. Lou Gehrig's disease. Motor Neuron Disease. MND. Doesn't matter what you call it. The effects are the same. You watch the person you love waste away in front of you. Like a fucking janitor. Walking round the building after everyone's gone home. Turning off the lights, one room at a time."

"I'm sorry. I didn't know."

Darren Gilman shrugged. "Nothing you can do. So

Gary says, 'Take all the time you need. Course I'll keep paying you. Just sign this, Daz. Keep the paperwork straight.' I was on medication wasn't I? Depressed, with what's happening to Linda. Like wading through fucking treacle. In the end I stopped taking it."

"But you signed the papers?"

"Yeah. Didn't have the strength to read them. 'Besides,' Gary says. 'If you can't trust your brother who can you trust?' But he's not paying me is he? It's a loan against my fucking shares. Two days after I buried my wife he asks for the money back. He knows full well I haven't got it. I haven't worked for three years. Re-mortgaged to pay for altering the house. Bathroom downstairs. So he puts his arm round my shoulder. 'No problem,' he says. 'Just sign your shares over.' He's my brother. Half-brother. Linda's not cold in the ground. And it's give him the shares or lose my house. Our house..."

A man who beats his wife and cheats his brother...

"So what do you do now?"

Darren Gilman shrugged. "Nothing. What can I do? Haven't worked for nearly five years now."

"Is that why you're selling the house?"

"Do I need the money you mean? No, mate. I'm off. Had enough of the bloody rain. And the memories..."

"Can I ask how well you knew Sarah Cooke?"

Gilman took time to reply. "How well does anyone know their brother's wife?" he said. "Better than most in my case. We were friends." He stared at Brady. "Not in that way."

"I'm sorry, Mr Gilman. I didn't mean to imply anything."

Did I imply anything? I don't think so...

"I'm just saying. That's all."

"Did you see her very often?"

"Like I said, we were friends. She used to phone me. I'd go round. We'd talk. And we had something in common, didn't we?"

"What sort of things did you talk about?"

"We didn't. We talked about one thing. Gary. At first I'd try and explain. Tell her that Gary didn't mean any harm. He'd always been like that. When he was younger. Hot-headed. A bit wild."

"Whereas you weren't?"

"No. Not me. I went to Cubs. Then Scouts. Got my badges."

"But then it changed. After your wife died..."

"What do you think? Course it bloody changed." Another stare. "How could it not fucking change?"

I'm done. Self-pity's kicking in. All her clothes are still in the wardrobe. Her teddy bear is still on the bed.

Brady closed his notebook and stood up. "Thank you, Mr Gilman. You've been really helpful."

"We were trying for a baby. What do you think of that? One day she's taking her temperature and getting excited. The next day she can't get the top off the marmalade."

"I'm sorry, Mr Gilman. I can't imagine how..."

What do I say?

"How difficult that must have been..."

"You married are you?"

Brady smiled. "No, not yet. June. Not much more than six months. I probably ought to start writing a speech."

Gilman looked at the empty space under the window. "May for us. Just as the cherry blossom was out. I planted a tree for her in the garden. She never saw it in bloom."

Brady paused in the doorway. *You're a shit if you ask this question. As sensitive as Gary Cooke. And if you don't ask it you're not doing your job...*

"I'm sorry, Mr Gilman. I forgot to ask. Just for the record obviously. Where were you the night Sarah Cooke was murdered?"

Gilman unfolded himself from the chair again. The cat sidled back into the room, determined to try his luck a second time. "I'll show you out," Gilman said. "And I was here, wasn't I? Where I am every Saturday night. Watching *Match of the Day*. And it was raining. So who's going out in that? And I wasn't feeling too good. Reheated a curry. Should know better by now."

"Thank you." Brady held his hand out. "I appreciate your time. And don't worry. I'll let myself out."

"Boss, can you spare me a minute?"

Jim Fitzpatrick looked at him. "I've a meeting with the Chief Constable in half an hour. I've a pile of paperwork to go through and I've a disciplinary to prepare for. But if it's a question I can answer in two minutes, ask me."

So forget the long introduction...

"Thanks, boss. You're interviewing someone. Does it make you suspicious if they get talkative?"

"You mean in response to your questions?"

"Yes. Give you too much detail."

"Alright," Fitzpatrick said. "Let me put it this way. If

you ask someone, 'Did you steal the apples?' and they answer 'no' then you *might* have a suspect. If you ask someone 'Did you steal the apples' and they say, 'I don't like apples and besides I didn't have a ladder to climb over the orchard wall and even if I did I'm scared of heights so I wouldn't have done it anyway and besides I was walking the dog when the apples were stolen...'" Fitzpatrick paused. "Then you've *definitely* got a suspect." He gave Brady a questioning look. "That do you?"

"Perfectly, boss. More than perfectly. Thanks."

So maybe there is another suspect. The problem is, I'm the only one who thinks so...

16

"Stan? Mike?" Jim Fitzpatrick was standing in the door of his office. "Conference room. Two minutes."

Bill Slater was already there. Eddie Harvey and Dave Elleray followed them in.

"This won't take long," Fitzpatrick said. "The guys in fingerprints say Gary Cooke's prints are all over the house. Ditto for DNA. None on the body sadly. But I've just had this..."

He tapped 'play' on the screen. The CCTV images flickered to life. "King Street?" Bulman said.

Fitzpatrick nodded. "Half a mile away. As close as we can get. Hang on... I need to fast forward."

Brady watched time speed up. A blur of late night cars and buses.

23:05. Fitzpatrick moved it back to normal speed. The cars and buses started behaving more sensibly.

"There," Fitzpatrick said. 23:06:27. A Porsche went through the picture.

"Can you freeze it, boss? Maybe see the number?"

"I've already tried, Stan. There, look." Fitzpatrick froze the screen. "That's when the car's at the best angle to the camera. But there's not enough light."

"But you can see the pattern," Brady said. "It's a personalised number plate."

Fitzpatrick nodded. "Two letters, four numbers. That's how I saw it."

"Presumably there's a techie down in the bowels of the building that can enhance it?" Bulman said. "But we don't need to. It'll be Gary Cooke's car. Red Porsche. GC 1899."

"They're already on it," Fitzpatrick said. "But like you say, Stan, we know what it's going to be. Throw in finger-prints all over the house, Mike's little old lady across the road, the incident before Christmas. Four boxes: four ticks. That's enough for me. Bill, anything we've missed?"

Slater shook his head. "No. Be nice to retire on a case we can win. No, nothing boss." He turned to Brady. "Looks like he didn't need her so much after all, eh?"

What about the brother? Maybe there's another suspect? But if you say anything...

"You don't think it's worth checking on the brother, boss? It all seems... I don't know. Too good to be true..."

Bulman laughed out loud. Slater consulted Heaven again. Fitzpatrick put it into words. "No, Mike, I don't. Manpower and resources. The rest of Manchester's villains don't go on holiday just because we're working on a murder. Sometimes we get an open goal. So let's kick the ball in the net. Stan, take Mike and go and get him. He's at the showroom now – "

"You know that for sure, boss?"

"Give me some credit, Stan. I just phoned. Said I wanted to buy a Merc. Could I pay cash? Gary Cooke doesn't know my voice and he seemed more than happy to help. So go and bring him in. Eddie, Dave, you go along as back up. Just in case."

"Arrest or questioning, boss?"

"Arrest, Stan. Let's put this one to bed. Give Bill his retirement present."

17

"Your first arrest," Bulman said. "Popping your cherry, old son."

"I've made plenty in uniform."

"They don't count. Some drunk falls over in front of you. It's hardly Inspector Morse, is it? Mind you, Clouseau could've solved this one. Prints all over the house. Let's go. Gary Cooke's a good lad, but murder's murder."

Bulman unlocked his car. Brady saw Eddie Harvey and Dave Elleray climbing into a squad car. Four of them to arrest one man...

"He's a big fucker," Bulman said, reading his thoughts. "Hope he comes quietly. My days of jumping over walls are behind me."

"We'll be fine," Brady said. "He's not going to make a fuss is he? Not going to do his business much good though."

"You're right there." Bulman reached across and opened the glove compartment. Pulled out a hip flask that looked like it had survived at least one war. Tilted it to his lips. "Into battle," he said. "You want some?"

"No, I'm fine," Brady said. "I won't pretend I'm not nervous but... Like you say, let's go."

Bulman pulled out onto the main road. Brady glanced in the wing mirror. Saw the squad car following them.

Let's talk about something else. At least for five minutes...

"How did it go?" he said. "Fitz said you had your medical the other day."

Bulman shrugged. "Same as it always goes. Stop drinking, stop smoking, lose weight, get some exercise."

"Makes sense. Stop drinking and stop smoking – you're going to live longer."

"No. It means it'll *feel* like longer. My nan's 98. She has five Woodbines a day and a glass of milk stout every night. It's in your genes. Not in what some bloody po-faced doctor tells you to do. Mind you – come on, mate, decide which bloody lane you're in – haven't felt too clever today. Teach me to have the fry-up in the canteen."

FIFTEEN MINUTES of stop-start Manchester traffic and they were there. A showroom between two cash-and-carry warehouses. A high security fence, a maroon and white sign. *Gary Cooke Cars.* A dozen very expensive cars parked outside.

"We're in the wrong job," Bulman said. "Work our bollocks off for 30 years and we still won't be anywhere near one of these cars."

Brady didn't reply. He could feel the nerves. His mouth was dry.

Does it get better? Ten years from now will I be relaxed about it? 'Anything special today, love?' 'No, not really. Arresting a murderer. But I'll be back in time for dinner...'

"Good start," Bulman said. "We don't even have to go inside." He pointed through the windscreen. Two men were standing by a bright red Porsche. One in overalls, one in a suit. The one they'd come to arrest...

'He's a big fucker.'

He was. Over six feet tall and built like a rugby player.

Yes, Stan, Let's hope he comes quietly.

Bulman parked the car. Brady climbed out, glanced back. No sign of the squad car.

"You want to wait for Eddie and Dave?"

"They'll be here in a minute," Bulman said. "Besides, we can't. Gary Cooke knows me. Can't make small talk about cars for five minutes and then say, 'Oh, by the way, Gary, you're under arrest...'"

"Fair point..."

They walked across the forecourt. Gary Cooke turned. Saw Bulman, looked surprised. "Morning, Stan, police pay gone up suddenly? Or have you won the lottery?"

Bulman shook his head. "Neither, Gary." He flicked his eyes towards the mechanic.

"Give us two minutes will you, John?"

Gary Cooke turned back to Bulman and Brady. "So what can I do for you?"

Bulman took a step forward. "Gary Cooke," he said.

I'm surprised. I thought he'd sound nervous. Arresting someone he knows...

"I am arresting you for the murder of Sarah Cooke. You do not have to say – "

Gary Cooke stared at Bulman. A look of disgust. Incredulity. As though Bulman had made an insultingly low offer for one of his cars.

"Don't be a prick, Stan."

"You do not have to say anything – "

"Are you serious, Stan? Fucking hell, you are. I'm phoning my – "

Cooke reached into his pocket. Bulman rushed forward. Tried to take hold of Cooke's arm. Brady saw Cooke brush him off like a child. "I'm phoning my solicitor, you fucking idiot."

"Someone can do that for you." Bulman was breathing heavily. Flushed. "We are arresting you for the murder of Sarah – "

"I didn't do it. She's the mother of my child, you clown."

"Fuck, Gary, your fingerprints are all over the house. So many fucking fingerprints I'm surprised you've got any left."

Does every arrest end up like this? An argument in a car park?

"Stan, I know you're a copper so I'll say this slowly. I – did – not – fucking – do – it."

"You're pissing me off now, Gary. For the third time, I am arresting you – "

Brady saw it. The moment Gary Cooke's temper snapped. Saw his eyes change. Saw his muscles clench. Saw the red mist descend. Finally understood what Sarah Cooke had lived through.

"And for the third fucking time – " Gary Cooke

stepped forward. Pushed Bulman squarely in the chest. Sent him sprawling into Brady " – I didn't do it."

Brady scrambled to his feet. Saw Stan Bulman still on the ground. Saw Eddie Harvey finally arrive. Saw Gary Cooke running across the car park.

Didn't think. Ran after him. Dodging between cars. Across ten yards of tarmac. Between two more cars. Saw people watching open mouthed through the office window. Ran down the side of the showroom.

Gary Cooke in front of him. Forty, 50 yards. Stopping. Opening a high, barred gate. Razor wire coiled along the top of it.

Someone must open it in the morning. Maybe some of the staff come in that way...

Gary Cooke running down the alley.

What are those? More warehouses?

Brady went through the gate after him.

Shoes. Black shoes to go with my suit. Useless for running. Need my trainers. Trainers and shorts...

Brady fleetingly noticed the warehouse signs. Saw the rubbish in the alley. Discarded pizza boxes, ripped black bin bags, an abandoned red stiletto, the heel broken.

Which way had he gone? Left. Cooke was 30, maybe 40 yards in front of him. Brady glanced back. No sign of Bulman. No sign of Eddie Harvey.

You and me then, Gary. And only one of us built like a rugby player...

Brady looked up. Cooke had stopped. Was standing facing him. A brick wall on his left. Rendered concrete on the opposite wall. The other stiletto in front of him.

Is he giving himself up? He can't be. What the hell's he doing?

Brady walked towards him.

Do I look confident? In control? I bloody hope so. I don't feel it. Hadn't realised how big he was.

Cooke was waiting for him. *Even taller than his brother.* Fair hair cut short. A square face. Four or five days' growth of beard. Broad shoulders.

Three years of mopping up on Friday and Saturday night and sitting in a classroom being fast-tracked. Now you're in an alley. Welcome to the real world, Brady.

The gap between them closed to ten feet. Brady stopped. Close enough.

And close enough to talk.

"Two things," Gary Cooke said. "I didn't do it. Yes, I hit her. But I loved her. She had my child. But something comes over me. I did not kill her. I'm trying to get help. You need to believe that."

The mist had lifted. Running down the alley. Something physical. The anger had gone.

Brady took a step closer. "You're under arrest," he said. "For the murder of Sarah Cooke. You do not have to say anything – "

Gary Cooke stared at him. "Piss off," he said. "I'm not under arrest. Not unless you've got more reinforcements than that fat bastard who can't keep up."

Brady risked a glance behind him.

Cooke laughed. "No reinforcements, mate. And you're not going to arrest me. You're barely old enough to shave."

"I've got no choice."

"Listen to me will you? I don't pretend to be a good person. Yes, I hit her. That doesn't mean I murdered her."

"Your prints are all over the house."

"Of course they are. My daughter lives there. Of course they bloody are."

You don't have a choice. You can't let him walk away.

Where the hell is Stan? Where's Eddie. What are they doing?

"You see?" Cooke said. "I'm not under arrest. Because I didn't do it. Find the real bloody killer."

"No," Brady said. "You *are* under arrest. This isn't some fucking game. You don't get to choose. I'm a police officer. You're under arrest."

Cooke moved towards him. One step. Two.

One more and he's in range.

Shouting now.

"You fucking idiot. Go and help Stan Bulman. Try and arrest me and I'm going to have to hit you. That'll put you in hospital and me in jail."

"You're already going to jail. Resisting arrest. Assaulting a police officer."

Cooke laughed again. "I don't think so. There's half a dozen people watching through that window. They all saw Bulman attack me. Self-defence. But you take one step closer and I have to do something. It's lose-lose. Think it through. Fuck off and help your partner. Or maybe..."

Gary Cooke suddenly took a step back. Looked at Brady. Nodded. A man who'd realised his mistake. He'd misjudged someone.

He reached into his pocket. Pulled out a wad of notes.

"How much, son? How much to turn round? Two hundred? Five hundred? What's your price?"

Cooke held the notes out in front of him.

Brady's turn. The red mist.

Three years waiting. My first case. And the bastard tries to bribe me...

"Never. Never in a million years. You're under arrest you – "

He rushed forward. Cooke skipped nimbly to the side. Drove his fist into Brady's midriff. Smashed a huge right hand – still clutching the notes – into the side of Brady's head.

Took Brady off his feet.

He crashed to the floor. Felt his head jerk back with the impact. Crack against the brick wall.

The world turned black for a split-second.

A rugby player who can box.

Rugby...

Tackle...

Brady forced himself to look up. Saw Cooke take a step away from him. Flung himself forward. Threw his arms round Cooke's ankles.

Clung on.

Felt Cooke try to kick free.

Held on even tighter.

Heard running feet.

Heard Eddie Harvey shouting.

Felt the blackness overtake him again...

18

"They got him?"

The paramedic – dark hair receding, beard turning grey, already looking weary at eleven in the morning – nodded at Brady. "If you mean did they arrest him, yes. We arrived at the same time as the cavalry. Took four of your lads."

Brady tried to smile. "Thanks. What about... Do you know anything about Stan?"

The paramedic shook his head. "Your partner? No. We passed the other crew as we were turning in. Blue light was on. That's all I can tell you." He stood up, stooping slightly inside the ambulance. "Anyway, you're my concern, Mike. Lie down on the bed. Let's get you comfy. We'll be there in ten minutes. Get you checked over."

"No." Brady struggled to his feet. "No, I'm fine. I've got to get back to work."

The paramedic shook his head. "Mate, you've been

knocked out. You were out for five minutes. You need an X-ray. You need checking."

"No."

I need to make sure Gary Cooke's been arrested. Need to find out how Stan is...

Brady sat back down on the bed. Waited for the dizziness to stop.

"I'll take Stan's car. Drive back."

The paramedic smiled. "Right. Good idea. You're completely fit to drive. And you'll have the keys. Or could they be in your mate's pocket?"

Brady nodded slowly. "OK. Fair point. I'll call a taxi."

"Call a psychologist is what you should do. Look, you're bleeding. You've got a bruise the size of an egg. You need checking."

Brady touched his fingers to the back of his head. *Two eggs more like.* Winced. Shook his head again. Stood up. Swayed. Managed to stay standing up. "I've got to get back."

The paramedic looked resigned. "I can't make you. But promise me something? Do that and we'll drop you off at the station. At least that way I can check on you for ten more minutes."

"Sure. What is it?"

"Go and do whatever it is you have to do. Be a hero. *Then* go and get checked. Explain the situation. Tell them you're a cop. You've been knocked out. They'll see you straightaway. And get someone to drive you."

Brady nodded. "Deal," he said.

The paramedic sighed. Spoke to his partner. "Greater

Manchester Police, Ali. And there's no need for the siren. This one's too tough for his own good."

"THANK YOU," Brady said. "I appreciate it."

"Remember what I said," the paramedic replied. "Do what you need to do. Then get yourself to A&E."

"I promise," Brady said, climbing carefully out of the ambulance.

HE PUSHED the office door open. Felt a wave of dizziness. Squeezed his eyes. Shook his head. Looked up, saw that the room was full. Jim Fitzpatrick at the front, speaking to the team.

"– So back to work, ladies and gentlemen. Whatever you were working on before. This one's done and dusted. Gary Cooke's – "

Jim Fitzpatrick stopped. Looked across the room. Saw Brady come in.

Heads turned. Tess Knightly. Eddie Harvey. Bill Slater – not gazing up to Heaven this time.

Brady saw Bill Slater stand up. Give him a nod. Start to clap. Tess joined in. Then Eddie. Then the whole room was clapping.

A room that looks like it needs some good news...

Jim Fitzpatrick smiled at him. "Well done, Mike. Bloody well done." He motioned for quiet, for everyone to sit down. "Eddie Harvey said you were hanging onto Cooke's ankles like a toddler hanging onto his mum."

There was good natured laughter. Some banter Brady didn't catch.

"Said you must have been a bloody awful two year old. But..."

Fitzpatrick held his hand up to cut off any more jokes. "Mike, you won't have heard. Stan Bulman's in hospital. He had a heart attack. We're waiting for news. So when this breaks up I need you in my office. Tell me what happened."

Brady nodded. "Yes, boss."

He reached out to move a chair so he could sit down. Felt the room start to spin. Closed his eyes, shook his head.

Felt the headache. A wave. Starting in the back of his skull. Flowing forward. Pulsing.

Put his hand on the back of a chair to steady himself. Felt a second wave. Nausea washing up from his feet. Felt the two waves crash headlong into each other.

Saw the floor rushing up to meet him. Felt a different pain.

Pain in his ribs as he crumpled onto the chair. The world spun faster. And then – for the third time – went black.

19

Brady opened his eyes. Blinked. Realised he was in bed. Saw Grace sitting at the end of it. Not his own bed...

Blinked again. Felt a wave of pain break against the back of his skull.

Looked around. Monitors. Wires connecting him to the monitors. Sides on the bed. "What happened?" he said.

Grace reached forward. Took his hand. Squeezed. Wiped away a tear. Smiled at him. A smile that even Brady could see was three parts worry to one part relief.

"You fainted at work," she said. "Blacked out they said."

Brady nodded. His mouth was dry. "Can you..."

Gesturing was easier. Grace passed him some water.

He tried to turn his head. Gave up because of the pain. Tried to sit up, found the pain was even worse. "What time is it?" he said.

"Nearly ten o'clock."

"Morning or night?"

"Night. That's why it's dark, darling. I've been here for three hours."

"Waiting for me to wake up?"

Grace nodded. "Watching you. Worrying."

The door opened. A man in his mid-30s. Scrubs. The obligatory stethoscope. Dark hair, glasses, a positive smile. But weary. One last patient before he could finally go home.

I've seen someone else who looked weary today. No. No idea...

"Mr Brady." He held out his hand. Brady reached forward to shake it. Grimaced with the pain. "I'm Rishabh Pujara."

"Michael, please."

Pujara nodded. "How are you feeling, Michael?"

Brady tried to smile. "I've felt better. My head. Ribs... Have I broken a rib?"

Pujara shook his head. "No. All your X-rays were clear. Where you fell at work and... One of your colleagues came with you in the ambulance. He said you'd been in a fight. This morning."

Brady nodded. Tried not to say too much in front of Grace. "A very short fight."

"You suffered a concussion. What happened at the police station was a delayed reaction. It's not uncommon. So I want you to rest. Try and sleep now. We'll talk tomorrow. Someone will be in to check on you."

"How long?" Brady said.

"In here? Three days at least. Off work? Until we are happy you can go back. At least a week. Probably a fortnight. People underestimate concussion at their peril."

Brady nodded again. Felt too weak to do anything else. "OK, Doctor. Talk in the morning."

Pujara smiled at him. A smile that took in Grace. "You have a dedicated nurse. Do as she tells you."

"And I'm telling you to do as you're told," Grace said as the door closed. "The job will still be there. And…" More tears. She made no attempt to wipe them away. "I don't want to lose you, Mike. I don't ever want to lose you."

"You won't, I promise…"

She nodded. "I had local radio on. The report said that a man had been arrested. And that someone else was in hospital."

Brady reached for her hand. Ignored the pain. Pulled her to him. "Stan Bulman. He had a heart attack. I told him we could – "

Grace put her finger on his lips. "Later," she said. "Tell me later. For now all I care about is you."

She kissed him as gently as she could. Stood up and reached for her coat. "I'm going now," she said. "So you can sleep. I'll come straight from work tomorrow. You make sure I find you in that bed. And remember, I love you."

Brady smiled at her. "I love you, Grace. And don't worry. I'll do as I'm told."

20

"I couldn't do this if you were a witness. But you've drawn the short straw. You're a copper – so I can."

Brady pulled himself upright in bed.

Jim Fitzpatrick sat down in the green hospital chair. "Tell me what happened yesterday."

"Where do you want me to start, boss?"

"From when you and Stan got to – "

The door opened. "Are you well enough to be kissed, Michael Brady? The bed was cold and lonely without you. I – oh... Sorry, I didn't – "

"Grace, this is my boss. Detective Chief Inspector Fitz-patrick."

Fitzpatrick laughed. Stood up and held his hand out. "Jim Fitzpatrick. And it's good to meet you at last."

Grace smiled back. Recovered her composure. "You too, Mr Fitzpatrick. And I'm guessing you need him to yourself for a few minutes?"

"If you don't mind. I don't want to sound rude but yes. I've some questions to ask him."

Grace nodded. "I'll walk slowly down the corridor to the coffee machine. Would you like one?"

Fitzpatrick shook his head. "No. Thank you for the offer. But I've reached the age where coffee from a vending machine takes its revenge. Usually at three in the morning."

"Bright girl," he said to Brady when Grace had gone. "But the coffee machine's not that far away. I need to know about the fight with Gary Cooke. And the rest. Better if Grace doesn't hear the details. Like I said to you before. You'll learn what to tell her. She'll learn what to ask."

"That's already happening."

"I know her father," Fitzpatrick said, raising his eyebrows. "That can't be easy for you. Law degree. Future father-in-law senior partner with one of Manchester's biggest solicitors. Some subtle pressure I'd imagine…"

Brady nodded. Wondered if the pain in his head would ever go. "Awkward as well, boss. If they're defending Gary Cooke."

"It happens, Mike. You know a solicitor… Sometimes they're on your side, sometimes they're not. Tell me what happened. She'll have decided what to have by now."

"We got to the showroom – Stan told me about his medical on the way – and Cooke's standing by his car talking to one of the mechanics. Stan said he needed to speak to him without the mechanic."

"Mechanic's name?"

"Cooke called him John."

"You'd recognise him again?"

Brady did his best to smile. "He might have more than

one mechanic called John. He won't have two with ginger hair."

"One in fifty according to the stats. Then what happened?"

"Stan arrested him. Or tried to arrest him. Cooke simply didn't believe him. Told him – both of us – to piss off. He reached into his pocket for his phone. Stan tried to grab his arm to stop him. Cooke just brushed him off."

"What was Cooke's attitude?"

"At that point? Arrogant. Dismissive. Like we were insulting him. Like we weren't worth taking seriously."

Fitzpatrick nodded again. "It won't be the last time you come across that. 'I'm too important to be arrested. Especially by someone like you.'"

"Stan is getting irritated by this point."

'And you're pissing me off now, Gary. For the third time, I am arresting you – '

"And then something snapped, boss. You could see it, like someone flicking a switch. Cooke lunges forward, pushes Stan in the chest. Stan crashes into me. We're both on the ground. I struggle to my feet and see Cooke running across the car park. And Eddie Harvey and Dave Elleray turning in."

"Stan's still on the ground here?"

"Yes, boss. He's... on his hands and knees. I made the decision to leave Eddie and Dave to look after him. And I went after Cooke."

Fitzpatrick nodded. "Fair enough, you're the closest to him. You chased him across the car park?"

"Yes. Down the side of the building. There was a gate.

Razor wire all over it. Some of the staff must come in that way in the morning. Through the gate, down the alleyway between the warehouses at the back. And then he stopped."

"Why?"

Brady shook his head. "Like he wanted to explain. Convince me he didn't do it. I was stupid. I'm sorry, I should have waited for Eddie and Dave. But..."

"But?"

"Something about him standing there. Just refusing to be arrested. The way he treated Stan. Like he thought we were idiots. Adrenalin. Then... Then he offered me a bribe."

Fitzpatrick nodded. "It won't be the last time that happens either. What did he say?"

'How much, son? How much to turn round? Two hundred? Five hundred? What's your price?'

"How much did I want to turn round? Walk away. He pulled a roll of notes out of his pocket. Offered me two hundred. Then five hundred."

"And you went for him?"

Brady shrugged. Winced at the pain in his ribs. "I think so. I must have done. I don't remember. I think... Maybe he hit me. The doctor said I hit my head on the wall as I fell back."

"That sounds about right. The bruise on your face is a good enough witness. But no real witnesses, Mike. Not until the cavalry comes round the corner and find you clinging to his leg."

"Like a toddler having a tantrum." Brady smiled ruefully. "What did they do with Stan?"

"Left him with someone. The office first-aider. As soon as they knew the ambulance was on its way."

"How is he now?"

"They say he's 'comfortable.' Whatever that means. But it's probably not my place to comment."

"Will you charge Gary Cooke?"

"With the extras?" Fitzpatrick shook his head. "I can't charge him with causing Stan's heart attack. There are no witnesses to what he did to you. There's no point. He'll get life for the murder. The judge won't give him a few extra days for you and Stan."

"You're certain he's guilty?"

"As certain as I can be. CCTV, fingerprints, eye witness. History of abuse. And temper. I'm sure we can find plenty of people to testify to that."

"He was... He was adamant he didn't do it," Brady said. "That's what seemed to be pissing him off. That we weren't bright enough to see he hadn't done it. That we'd – I don't know, maybe I'm speculating – taken the easy way out."

"We haven't," Fitzpatrick said, getting to his feet as Grace came back with her coffee. "And the Gary Cookes of this world are always certain they're right. Take care of him," he said to Grace.

Then he turned back to Brady. "Your Get-out-of-Jail card. No-one's ever lost it as fast as you did. I've never given it back either. Not until now. And one other thing, Mike..."

"Yes, boss?"

"Do as you're told. I might be a DCI but I'm easily outranked by the woman you're going to marry."

21

Jim Fitzpatrick stood up. Told Grace he'd see her again, no doubt.

"He seems nice," Grace said, giving Brady a look that wasn't open to misinterpretation. "And *extremely* intelligent. 'Do as you're told.'"

"Yeah, as bosses go I could have done a lot worse."

"So what was he talking about? Getting your 'Get-out-of-Jail' card back?"

And there's me thinking she might not ask...

"You really want to know?"

"Yes, darling." Grace stood up. Picked up his water jug. Ran the cold tap. "That's why I'm asking."

She always does that. She really wants to know something, she pretends it's not important. Turns her back. Asks me while she's doing something else. Six months' time. Love, honour, cherish – and tell the truth. As long as it doesn't make her worry...

"OK. Fitz – "

"Fitz? That's a bit familiar for a lowly Detective Constable. *Acting* Detective Constable."

"It's what everyone calls him. He told me he gives everyone a Get-out-of-Jail card. You can use it once. One major cock-up. The second time you're in trouble."

Grace put the full water jug back by his bed. "And you lost yours?"

"Yes. In record time. For going into Sarah's house on my own. And I probably came close to it for having coffee with her."

"What did he say?"

'You were stupid on Saturday night. Beyond stupid. And I don't like stupid coppers on my team. You could have fucked the investigation before it had started.'

"He said I'd made a mistake."

"And now you've redeemed yourself." Grace leaned carefully over the bed and kissed him. "You're a hero. I'm proud of you."

"According to the station gossip I was clinging on to Gary Cooke like a toddler clinging on to its mother. That doesn't sound very heroic."

Brady looked at her. The hint of green in her eyes. The way she smiled. 'Punching above your weight' didn't even come close.

He saw her pull the rugby shirt over her head. Saw her bra fall to the floor. Realised he might be feeling better.

"Come here," he said. "Come and lie next to me for two minutes."

"I can't. The wires, the monitors."

"You're alright. I'm not hooked up any more. And if I

was someone would come running. Come here. I need to hold you."

He shuffled over in the bed. Made room for her. Winced. Hoped she hadn't noticed.

"Kick your shoes off."

"I'll have to lie on the side of the bed. There'll be a lump of cold metal digging into me."

"Just like the bed in my flat then. You're getting old, Gracie..."

"Talking of old – that's not very fair of me – Mum and Dad send their love."

Don't spoil it, Grace. Don't talk about your parents now...

"And Dad says have you thought about the conversation on Christmas Day? The one you didn't tell me about..."

"No. Because we've had the conversation before. And we'll have it again."

"He only wants what's best for you."

No, Grace, he wants what's best for you. What he thinks is best for you. Marry a solicitor. Or an accountant. Not a lowly copper who grew up in Whitby and went to the local comprehensive...

"This is what's best for me," Brady said.

"Lying in a hospital bed because someone's pushed your head into a brick wall?" Grace sat up. "What about me, Mike?"

Don't react. She's upset. Worried. Don't say the wrong thing...

"This is what I am, Grace. This is all I've ever wanted to do. I'm sorry. I can't be a solicitor. I... "

"What?"

Don't say the wrong thing...

"I'd be bored. I'm sorry."

"So now my father's boring? Christ, Michael, at least no-one pushes a solicitor's head into a brick wall. And he wasn't boring when he gave us the money for the deposit was he?"

Brady reached out for her. She pulled away. "Grace, I didn't say that, I didn't mean..."

"I'm going, Mike. I need some fresh air. I can't stand seeing you like this. And you need to sleep. We'll talk tomorrow."

"Grace, don't be silly..."

The door closed behind her.

How the hell did that happen?

22

Brady had less than two minutes to dwell on it. The door opened again.

"Doctor Pujara, I thought you'd have gone home by now."

He must have passed Grace in the corridor. Was she crying? Would he have noticed?

Pujara smiled. "Soon. But... I had to come and see you, Michael."

He looks like he's come to deliver bad news. The X-rays. They've made a mistake. My skull's fractured. They need to operate...

"I can tell it's bad news," Brady said. He pulled himself upright. "Don't try and dress it up, Rishabh. Just tell me the worst."

Should I phone Grace? Get her back? No, wait until I know what it is. Maybe there'll be something else I shouldn't tell her...

"It's the worst part of our job," Pujara said. "Yours as

well, I imagine. Although maybe you haven't had to do it yet?"

What's he talking about? Coppers don't deliver medical –

"We thought you would want to know straightaway. I'm sorry," Rishabh Pujara said. "There is never a way to soften the blow. Your colleague, Mr Bulman. He died this afternoon. I'm very sorry, Michael."

'Stan? I want you to take Mike Brady out with you this morning.'

"When?" Brady said. "How?"

"Late this afternoon. A second heart attack. There was nothing we could do. It was very quick."

'Don't make it personal. You liked her. I could tell. Don't. You let it get personal, you take it home with you. Sooner or later it fucks up your marriage. And your judgement.'

He taught me more than I realised...

"Do people know? His wife... The station?"

Pujara nodded. "His wife, obviously. I think someone was letting your colleagues know. Are you alright, Michael? Do you want someone with you?"

'I'm going, Mike. I need some fresh air. You need to sleep. We'll talk tomorrow.'

"No. I'm fine, Rishabh. I'll be OK. I'll phone my girl-friend. Tell her. Thank you for letting me know."

Brady held his hand out. Pujara shook it. "Again, I'm sorry. You're sure you'll be alright?"

"Yes, really. I'm fine. I'll try and get some sleep."

'You're pissing me off now, Gary. For the third time, I am arresting you – '

And then Stan was lying on the ground. I was chasing Gary Cooke. I should have stayed with him...

Brady reached for his phone. Then stopped.

I shouldn't tell her. Not tonight. We had an argument because she was worried. I can't make it worse...

'No-one pushes a solicitor's head into a brick wall.' *You're right, Gracie. And no-one shoves a solicitor over and gives him a heart attack...*

23

Brady lay back on the pillows. Stared at the ceiling. Tried to push the argument with Grace out of his head.

Failed.

Tried to push the image of Stan Bulman out of his head.

Failed with that one as well.

Tried again. Grace grudgingly took a step back.

Sarah's dead. Stan's dead. Who killed her? Think it through. You owe it to Stan.

He saw Gary Cooke standing in the alley. Face to face.

"*I didn't do it. Yes, I hit her. But I loved her. She had my child. But something comes over me. I did not kill her. I'm trying to get help. You need to believe that.*"

Heard Jim Fitzpatrick.

'*Throw in fingerprints all over the house, Mike's little old lady across the road, the incident before Christmas. Four boxes: four ticks.*'

Heard him a second time...

'*You want to catch a killer, Michael? You've got to think*

like a killer. You've got to be the killer. And the victim. You've got to get inside their heads. And when you've finished killing – or being killed – you've got to go round Tesco with your wife.'

Brady leaned across. Poured himself some water. Lay back again. Wondered how the ceiling tile – fourth row, third one from the window – had got that ominous brown stain.

I'm Sarah Cooke. Alone in the house. Gary's outside. If I let him in he's going to hit me. If I don't let him in... He put a spade through the car window. What else is he capable of? So she phones me. But she must know I'm no match for Gary Cooke. She's not thinking straight.

Neither is Grace.

Stop it. Sort it out in the morning.

Sarah Cooke phones me because she wants someone who'll believe her. Take her seriously.

The door opened again: Brady's favourite nurse. "Anisa, how are you?"

Black hair, dark brown eyes, the widest smile Brady had ever seen. "Michael... You're supposed to be asleep. I was just checking on you. You want me to get you something? Help you sleep?"

"No. I'm thinking. Trying to work out a murder."

Anisa laughed out loud. "Planning or solving? You let me know. That man of mine. If he didn't get those kids to bed when I told him..."

"All you have to do is smile at the jury, Anisa. You'll get off. You on duty all night?"

She nodded. "Just me. Leah's helping out in materni-ty." She pointed at the ceiling. "Next floor up. So just me

until six in the morning. Then go home, fix some breakfast an' try an' sleep. You want anything? Water?"

"No thanks. Grace fixed it for me before she went."

"OK. You need me, you know where I am."

"Thanks. I'll try and sleep."

Anisa moved towards the door. "Anisa – "

"What's the matter, Michael?"

"Do you know about Stan Bulman? The other
policeman?"

She nodded. "I heard. Some time this afternoon. You
sure you don't want something to help you sleep?"

"I'm sure."

"OK. You take care, Michael. An' you know where
I am."

SHE CLOSED THE DOOR. Brady went back to staring at the
ceiling.

*She phones me because she knows I can get there quickly.
But what am I supposed to do? Nothing. She's just not thinking
straight.*

*Gary Cooke parks his car across the road. Slams the door.
Clearly in a bad mood. Walks across the road. What did Irene
Jefferson say? 'A big man. An aggressive way of walking.'*

*'You want a sign? I'll give you a sign. Strangulation.'
Sarah kept her scarf on when we had coffee...*

*'If someone's strangled by a partner they're seven times
more likely to be murdered by the same partner.'*

Brady stared at the brown stain.

Knew he was missing something.

Had no idea what he was missing.

Midnight came and went.

Grace and Stan Bulman were frequent visitors.

Rain started beating against the window.

One last effort, Brady. Come on.

'Catch a killer, Michael? Think like a killer. Be the killer.'

Put yourself in Gary Cooke's head. Saturday night, you drive round there. Why? Surely you've better things to do on a Saturday night than worry about your ex-wife? But you still love her. Or you say you do.

What did Angie say? 'She needs him. Money, somewhere to live maybe. And in his own fucked-up way he needs her.'

So what do you want, Gary? Not to see your daughter. You know she's not there. So it's Sarah. But what did you want? What did you want when you put the spade through the car window?

And why kill her? Why kill her on that Saturday night? Is it like Stan said? She provoked you? Finally went too far?

You tick every box, Gary. But none of it makes sense.

Brady sighed. Listened to the rain. Accepted that he still hadn't found the missing piece of the jigsaw. Accepted that sleep was never going to come.

You've been a detective for two weeks. You're in hospital. Your partner's dead. You've fallen out with the woman you love. You think the wrong person's been arrested – but you're too stupid to work it out.

'What did you do at college anyway?'

'I read law.'

'Law? Then you're an idiot. Why didn't you become a solicitor? Nice suits. Fuck off to the pub on Friday lunchtime...'

Maybe Stan had been right.

Maybe Grace's father was right...

24

Brady pushed the covers back. Levered himself carefully out of bed. Reached for his dressing gown. Opened the door and walked down the corridor to the nurses' station.

"Anisa?"

"Michael? What are you doing out of bed? You want something to help you sleep? You should have pressed the buzzer."

Brady shook his head. "No, I don't want to sleep. I've been lying awake. Thinking."

Anisa smiled at him. "Missing your girlfriend? You feeling better all of a sudden?"

Brady smiled ruefully. "The second one? Maybe. The first one? Yes, but we had an argument."

Anisa shook her head. "Michael, you need to sort it out. Send her a text. Never go to bed on an argument. You want a cup of tea?"

"Please," Brady said. "I was sort of hoping you were making tea."

"I'll make a deal," Anisa said. "You go and text your girlfriend. Your first argument?"

"First one this serious."

"Right, so she'll still be awake. You do that and I'll make you a cup of tea. I'll trust you. But no text, no tea."

Brady knew she was right. "Deal," he said and walked back to his room.

"You do that for me?" Anisa said five minutes later.

"Yeah. And you were right. She was awake. She's going to call in tomorrow morning. On her way to work."

"That's good. And you remember what I said. Make friends before you go to bed. What were you arguing about anyway? No, you don't have to tell me."

Brady laughed. "You made the tea. Nothing really. Well, her father's a solicitor. Senior partner. Wants me to work for him."

Anisa looked at him over the top of her mug. "An' you want to be a policeman."

"It's all I've ever wanted to do. I did law at university. But only because I thought it would help. Give me an understanding. You know..."

"An' your girlfriend doesn't like to see you hurt. She's going home thinking you could have been killed. Thirty years of worry stretching in front of her..."

"Yeah. I guess so. But... This is who I am, Anisa. This is all I can do."

Brady sipped his tea. He'd wondered why half the guys at the station were married to nurses. Now he understood. Cups of tea in the middle of the night. Shared experiences. Shared scars.

"How did you meet her?" Anisa said.

"In a café. She'd left her book behind. I picked it up and started reading. You know, like a lot of cafés have books lying around for people to read. She came back. We started talking…"

"Hey, that's romantic. I like that. What was the book?"

"*Tess of the d'Urbervilles.* Thomas Hardy."

"Ah… We did that at school. Poor old Tess."

"What about you?"

Cops and nurses. The middle of the night. Sharing a cup of tea. Someone to talk to…

"Me? Don't make me laugh. Someone will complain I woke them up. Me? I married the wrong man."

"Oh, I'm sorry. I didn't mean…"

This time Anisa didn't even try to stop herself laughing. "No, bless you. I'm feeling down. I've broken up with a boyfriend. My friend… She says, 'Why don't you come out, girl?' I say no. She says, 'I've found you Mr Right, honey. Good job, funny, smokin' hot…' So I go. Mr Right has injured himself playing football. But he's sent a substitute. So I'm the girl who married Mr Wrong."

"But it worked?"

"Sure did. He wasn't smokin' hot but he was kinda cute. An' he's a good man. Fifteen years, three children. Maybe he was Mr Right all along."

25

Brady finished the last of his tea. Someone had pressed their buzzer. Anisa had hurried off to do whatever needed doing at one in the morning. Brady had taken his tea back to his room.

My own room. Police perks...

He climbed back into the bed as carefully as he'd climbed out of it. Wondered when Rishabh Pujara would let him go home.

He reached over and turned his light off. But he was in a hospital. It was never dark: never silent.

So deal with it. Find a way of going to sleep. They'll be waking you up for breakfast in ten minutes...

I'll have to go and see Stan Bulman's wife. Tell her what happened. And tell her we've found the killer.

Brady heard footsteps outside his room.

Someone else needing Anisa...

Now Stan Bulman was on his hands and knees in the car park. Brady forced the image out of his head. Made himself concentrate.

She phones me because she knows I can get there quickly. But she knows I can't do anything. She's just not thinking straight.

Why is she not thinking straight? Because she's terrified.

Why is she terrified?

Because Gary Cooke is outside.

How does she know it's Gary Cooke?

She's seen the car. Or she's recognised the noise of the car door slamming. Or he's shouted to her.

Did he ring her? Text her? No, they didn't find anything on her phone.

More footsteps outside the room.

Anisa back from her patient.

Anisa...

What did she say?

'*So I go. Mr Right has injured himself playing football. But he's sent a substitute. So I'm the girl who married Mr Wrong.*'

Supposing Sarah Cooke saw Mr Wrong?

Supposing it wasn't Gary Cooke?

Brady turned the light back on. Ignored the pain. Swung his legs out of bed. Stood up. Walked round the bed to his window. Stared through the rain.

Rain. Fog. You couldn't recognise anyone. You saw the person you expected to see.

It was one of the overflow car parks, only two cars in it now. Brady looked around. Found his jeans. Pulled them on over his pyjama bottoms. Reached for his dressing gown. Opened the door, walked down to the nurses' station. Anisa looked up.

"Michael, what on Earth are you doing? Hospitals have beds for a reason..."

There's no other way to say this...

"I'm going outside for two minutes."

Anisa looked at him. Jeans, dressing gown, slippers. "You're joking, right? You think I'll make you another cup of tea if you promise to go back to bed?"

Brady shook his head. "No. I need to test something. A theory."

Anisa shook her head. "Michael, whatever you're thinking, the answer is 'no.' You've been concussed. Go back to bed."

"You trusted me half an hour ago. I need to stand in the car park. And for you to look out of the window..."

Anisa shook her head again. More forcibly this time. "No. Go back to bed, Michael. You've been concussed. Knocked out. An' I'd lose my job."

"Two minutes, Anisa. Just so you can look out of the window and see if you recognise me."

"Right, Michael. Like there's going to be more than one concussed madman standing in the car park in the pouring rain?"

The buzzer rang. Anisa gave Brady a warning look.

He raised his eyebrows. Smiled at her. "Someone needs you. And if you didn't know I'd gone outside..."

"You're making me an accomplice."

"What to?"

"Stupidity, Michael."

The buzzer rang again.

"I have to answer that," Anisa said. "I'm going to look in your room as I come back. I expect you to be in bed."

Brady watched her walk down the ward. Sent a small prayer of thanks to whoever needed water. Or a bedpan.

She's right. It's stupid. Supposing she calls your bluff? Supposing she doesn't look out of the window? But there's no alternative. You've got a theory? Test it. Go and get wet.

He pushed the door of the ward open. Realised this was the furthest he'd walked in two days.

Only down one flight of stairs. Surely I can walk down one flight of stairs...

There was a grey security door at the bottom. By Brady's reckoning it opened straight on to the car park.

Maybe it's the consultants' car park. Maybe they've got fobs to open it from the other side...

Brady didn't have a fob. And he didn't want to risk walking all the way round the hospital to the main entrance. Going out or coming back in...

He pressed the lever in the middle of the door. Opened it slightly. Saw the rain in the lights from the car park. Looked around. Nothing to wedge the door open with. Nothing except...

Michael Brady took his slippers off. Bent down and placed them across the corner of the door frame. Stepped out into the rain. Pulled the door almost closed behind him. Walked barefoot across the hospital car park. Turned round and looked at the window of his room. Gambled that he'd see an angry nurse looking down at him.

LOST HIS BET.

Felt the rain running down his back.

Felt the wet tarmac under his bare feet.

'This is what I am, Grace. This is all I've ever wanted to do. I can't be a solicitor. I'd be bored.'

So I'm standing in a car park in the rain. Waiting for a nurse who's got far more important things to do than look out of a window and –

Maybe not. Brady saw a face at the window.

Anisa? Yes, because I know it's Anisa. Could I swear it was Anisa in front of a jury? No.

Brady waved. An arm waved back. He ran for the door. Retrieved his slippers. Walked back up the flight of stairs. Told himself he was feeling dizzy because he was tired. Told Anisa he'd always be in her debt.

"So…" he said.

"Did I recognise you? Yes, like I said – "

"But supposing you hadn't known it was me?"

"Then no. I could tell it was a man. I could tell how old you were. Roughly. But if I hadn't known it was you… No."

"Thank you. That's all I wanted."

"So it was worth getting wet?"

Brady smiled, "Yes. And thank you again."

"You look cold. You want another cup of tea?"

"No, you've done enough. More than enough for me."

She shook her head. "You're mad. But I'm glad it's not me you're chasing. Make sure you get good an' dry before you get into bed."

Brady did as he was told. Fell back onto the pillows.

Knew exactly what he had to do in the morning.

Finally, finally slept.

26

Anisa put her head round the door. "Just checking before I go home. Making sure you haven't caught pneumonia."

Brady laughed. "I'm fine. I've been awake since about five."

"Thinking?"

"Always thinking." Brady looked upwards. "And checking that brown stain isn't getting any bigger. Did you say it was maternity up there?"

Anisa winked at him. "It's blood, honey. From the men who faint and fall over. You sure you're OK?"

My head hurts. I'm still feeling dizzy. But I know what I have to do. And I'm not going to do it lying in bed...

"I'm good. My ribs are still sore. But I'm getting better."

"No headaches? No dizziness?"

Brady shook his head. "None at all."

. . .

'*Keep the numbers. You'll have more contacts than any man has a right to have. Your wife will pick up your phone and think you're having an affair. But keep the numbers. You think a witness has nothing more to tell you. Something changes – and he's the one person you need to talk to. And fast.*'

She, not he. But thanks, Stan...

"Miss Jefferson. Good morning. It's Michael Brady. Detective Constable Michael Brady. I spoke to you – "

"I remember who you are, Detective Constable. I'm hardly likely to forget, am I? It's not every day the person across the road is murdered."

"That's what I wanted to ask you about, Miss Jefferson. Just a couple of points I'd like to check."

Brady could hear her moving around. It sounded like she was in the kitchen.

What's that? Biscuits falling into a bowl? Feeding the dog? She seemed more of a cat person. Do cats eat biscuits?

He had no idea.

"When I spoke to you, Miss Jefferson, you mentioned the car."

"Yes, a foreign sports car. Parked right outside my house."

"You're sure about that. Outside your house? On *your* side of the road?"

"Absolutely sure. Then I watched him walk across the road. Such an aggressive way of walking. Shoulders hunched. Then he came back to the car."

"Like he'd forgotten something?"

"Exactly like that. Twice."

"You're sure about that?"

"I may be old, Detective, but I can still count. 'How

can anyone forget something twice?' I said as much to Caesar."

"Caesar?"

"My cat, Detective. But you see it on Agatha Christie all the time. People distracted when they're planning a murder..."

"But you didn't see him carrying anything?"

"No. But you wouldn't, would you? You don't need a lot of equipment to strangle someone, Detective."

Brady thanked her. Apologised for ringing so early. Promised he'd let her know what happened in the case. Pressed the red button to end the call. Wondered if Caesar had enjoyed his biscuits.

Went back to staring at the ceiling.

Why would I park my car on the wrong side of the road?

Why would I go back to it a second time?

He could only think of one answer.

27

Someone else who was up and about early.

"Angie, good morning. It's Michael Brady. I saw you the other day – "

"The man on the silver unicorn. What can I do for you before I've even had a coffee?"

"Answer me a question. I think I already know the answer but…"

"You'd like it confirming?"

"If you don't mind."

"Go on then."

"You said that abuse is triggered – or it increases – if someone thinks they're losing control. That it can escalate. Maybe the woman is moving away. Starting a new relationship."

"Yes. I've seen it happen a hundred times."

"Supposing it's the man that's moving away? Supposing something changes in the man's life?"

"Are you talking about someone going to prison? Here's something to remember me by?"

"No," Brady said. "Supposing he's moving away? Moving to a different part of the country. Won't see her again?"

Angie was silent for a moment. No sounds of a cat being fed. "It's unusual," she said. "I can't think of a time that's happened. Prison, yes. It happens when someone's out on bail – usually despite our best efforts. Knows they're likely to go down. 'Here, love, something to remember me by. In case you're thinking of seeing anyone else while I'm inside.' But Joe Average, because he's being transferred to Aberdeen? I've not come across it."

"But not impossible?"

Angie's cynical laugh was back. "You know the saying? Behind every great man there's a great woman? My experience is slightly different. Behind every woman who walks through my door there's a fucked-up man who's put her there. So no, nothing's impossible. But..."

"But what?"

"Don't overthink it. Men are simple creatures. Don't credit them with too much intelligence."

Two DOWN, two to go.

And I'll have to wait. They won't be open at eight in the morning.

Brady levered himself out of bed. Walked across to the mirror. He needed a shave. Needed to wash his hair. Time enough...

He opened the drawer by the side of the bed. The

clothes he'd been wearing when he came in. Slowly, carefully, dressed himself.

The pain's manageable. Just don't stretch on your left hand side...

There was a knock on the door. "Goodness me, Michael. What are you doing dressed?"

"Morning, Phyllis. The doctor said I could get some exercise today. Just walking round the car park. Can't do that in my dressing gown can I?"

Phyllis laughed. "Well eat your porridge first. Do you want some marmalade with your toast? And shall I put you down for porridge tomorrow?"

Brady said sure, he was getting addicted to it. Vowed he'd never eat porridge again in his life.

Eight-thirty. They must be open by now.

Brady dialled the number.

"Elliot's Estate Agents. How can I help you?"

"Morning, I hope you can. I bumped into an old friend of mine the other day. Darren Gilman? He told me his house was for sale through you. I was round there once. We're getting married in the summer. It would be perfect for us..."

"I'm really sorry, Mr... I'm sorry, I didn't catch your name. Mr... "

"Fitzpatrick."

"I'm sorry, Mr Fitzpatrick. I've been off for a few days but I'm almost certain contracts have been exchanged."

"Definitely? Would you check for me? My wife's expecting our first child. We wanted to move before the baby's born. And the house is just round the corner from her mother."

"Let me check for you. I'll just put you on hold."

There was a brief moment of silence. The sounds of someone flicking through paper. "Not just exchanged, Mr Fitzpatrick. They're actually completing today. My colleague's left a note. The vendor's dropping the keys in this morning."

"And someone else is moving in?"

"Yes." She laughed. "That's what happens at completion. Someone moves out. You move in. Hopefully before your wife has the baby. We've some other houses in the same area, Mr Fitzpatrick. One in particular..."

But Brady wasn't listening.

'The vendor's dropping the keys in this morning.'

Darren Gilman wasn't just moving.

He was moving today.

'No, mate. I'm off. Had enough of the bloody rain. And the memories...'

Brady stood up. Walked over to the window. Looked out. Saw himself in the car park. Saw Anisa wave. Seeing who she expected to see. Saw Irene Jefferson looking out of her window. Sarah Cooke...

All of them. Seeing who they expected to see...

Finally understood exactly what had happened.

He didn't say, 'I'm moving.'

He said, 'I'm off.'

Brady knew what he had to do. Knew there was no time to waste.

He phoned the office.

28

"June? Morning, it's Michael Brady ... from hospital, yes ... well, I've just eaten the hospital porridge so I could be on the critical list in the next half hour. Is the boss in?"

"He's not, Mike. He's out with the Chief Constable all day. Local politicians as well, I think. But I've just seen Tess Knightly going upstairs if she's any use to you?"

"That's fine. Thanks, June. See you soon."

Coming out of the refuge. 'Do you think he did it?'

'Gary Cooke? No, I don't think he did it. I know he did it.'

Maybe it would have been easier to persuade Jim Fitzpatrick...

"Tess? Hi, it's Michael Brady."

"Ah, our Hero of the Month. Shouldn't you be eating grapes and watching daytime TV?"

It's the same as always. There's no other way. Just come right out and say it.

"We've arrested the wrong man, skip. Gary Cooke didn't do it. His brother – half-brother – did it. Darren Gilman. And his house sale completes today."

There was silence at the other end of the phone. Then...

"June said you wanted to talk to Fitz. This is what you were going to tell him? That he's arrested the wrong man?"

There's no other way...

"Yes."

He'd thought Angie could be sarcastic. "So, Acting Detective Constable Brady – recent recipient of a blow to the head – you'd like me to explain to Detective Chief Inspector Fitzpatrick – regular recipient of yet another commendation – that he's wrong and you're right."

"Yes."

"And that the evidence – fingerprints, witnesses, CCTV, all the usual police bollocks – is wrong because you, lying in your hospital bed, have devised a cunning plan."

"Yes."

Tess Knightly sighed. "OK, I have a shitload of paperwork to do. But this is an entertaining start to the day. And because I admired your courage and you didn't make a total arse of yourself at the refuge, I'll give you thirty seconds to convince me. Twenty-nine..."

You've got one shot. One shot only.

"Why would you slam your car door three times?" Brady said.

"I thought we decided he'd forgotten something?"

"Sure. We've all done that. But you go back to your car and get whatever you've forgotten. Shut the car door once more. And what had he forgotten? Like Irene Jefferson said, how much equipment do you need to strangle someone?"

"OK, that's won you another thirty seconds..."

"And why did he park on the wrong side of the road?"

"Parking space? Expensive car – maybe he wanted to park under a streetlight?"

"No. There was plenty of space. It's a street where everyone parks on their drive."

"So what are you saying?"

"I'm saying he wanted to be seen, Tess. I'm saying he banged the car door three times to attract attention. I'm saying he parked across the road so Sarah Cooke would see the car if she was upstairs. I'm saying it was Darren Gilman, not Gary Cooke. And he wanted her to be terrified. So she'd let him in. So her defences would be down..."

"Why does he want to kill her?"

She's forgotten my thirty second time limit...

"Because his wife's dead. Because his brother's cheated him. Because he's stopped taking his medication. And because he's going to Spain this afternoon."

"What do you mean 'he's going to Spain?'"

"His house is for sale. He completes today. I spoke to the estate agent. I don't know if he's going to Spain. Portugal maybe. That's my bet. He doesn't look like a man who speaks French."

"Do I look like a woman who speaks French, putain? Three summers picking grapes. Don't judge a book by its cover."

Tess went silent. Brady knew she was weighing it up. The chances of looking like an idiot – of having to explain herself to Fitzpatrick – against the small possibility he might just be right.

"And that's your theory? The guy who's abused her for years didn't do it. The guy who's never touched her did do it?"

"Yes. For revenge. Maybe she rejected him. Because if Gary Cooke was going to kill her, why did he do it on *that* Saturday night?"

"What about the car? Gary Cooke's car is on CCTV."

"No. A dark coloured Porsche is on CCTV. We couldn't see the number plate. Even the techies couldn't make it out."

More silence.

Take as long as you need. You know I'm right. Might be right...

"OK. Just on the off-chance that there's a pig flying past the office window with Elvis on its back, I'll make a deal with you."

This is as good as you're going to get...

"I'll get someone to check the flight lists. Manchester Airport to Spain and Portugal. The next three days."

"It'll be today."

"Right. If he's on there, we'll bring him in for questioning. If he's not, get back into bed. And this conversation never took place."

Trust her. She's experienced. Don't press it...

"I want to be there."

"What?"

"I want to come with you."

"Don't be stupid, Brady. You're in hospital."

"I'll discharge myself. The hospital's on your way. Ring me, skip. I'll come down."

He could see her. Standing in the office shaking her head. Another man without a brain in his body...

"Your police pension, Brady."

"What about it?"

"Nominate me as the beneficiary, will you? You're not going to live long enough to draw it. And this isn't going to take long. If I haven't rung you in fifteen minutes go back to bed. Settle down with *Reader's Digest* like a good boy. But if he's on a flight I'll be waiting downstairs."

"Thank you."

"You're welcome. Remember to take your pyjamas off."

"I've already done it."

Fifteen minutes...

Brady sat down on his bed. Stood up ten seconds later. Stared out of the window.

Will we get there in time? What happened when Grace and I moved in? We turned up at lunchtime. Started unloading. Didn't have any food. Ate a takeaway...

He checked his watch.

Five minutes. Who's doing the checking? How long does it take to check flight records? We'll need authorisation. But this is a murder...

Six minutes.

His door opened.

"Grace..."

"Michael. I'm sorry about last night. I... "

Grace stopped. Stared open-mouthed. "You're dressed. What are you doing, Mike? Why are you dressed?"

'The doctor says I can go for a walk.'

I could say that. But one look at me and she'd know I was lying. So tell her the truth. That she's marrying someone who thinks the job is more important than his health. Who'll do whatever it takes. Whatever it costs...

"I'm waiting for Tessa to phone me."

"Tessa?"

"Tess Knightly. She's a DS. I told you. I wanted to speak to the boss. But he's out all day. We've arrested the wrong man. The real killer – I can't say..."

Grace shook her head. "This is insanity. Madness. One, how the hell do you know you've arrested the wrong man? Two. You are not the only bloody copper in Manchester. You are, though, the only one in bed with concussion. Because someone smashed your head into a brick wall."

Brady saw the tears. Saw her make no attempt to stop them. Knew he could live for ever and never feel more guilty...

"And – damn it, Mike – you're the only one I'm going to marry. The only one I care about."

...Until she said that.

"I'm sorry, Grace. I just have... I have to be there. Tess is checking flight times now. He's going to Spain. He killed her and he's going to Spain."

"And you've worked all that out have you? You? Lying in your hospital bed?"

"Grace, I'm sorry. It sounds stupid. I know it does. But yes, I have."

"It sounds more than stupid, Michael Brady. It sounds – "

Brady's phone rang. He glanced at his watch.

Nine minutes.

He looked up at Grace. "I have to answer this."

She stared back at him. One part fear, one part exasperation, one part resignation. "I love you, Michael Brady. I love you with every breath in my body. But there's a part of you that frightens me."

"I love you too, Grace. You know that. But – "

"Don't give me that 'this is who I am' crap, Mike. Just answer your bloody phone."

He pressed the green button.

"Astonishing. Bloody astonishing. Barcelona. Two-thirty this afternoon. Which means he needs to be at the airport by Twelve-thirty. I'll be outside in five minutes."

"I'll be downstairs."

Brady looked at Grace. "I've never loved you more than I love you this minute."

"Just go, Michael. But tell me one thing."

"Anything. What is it?"

"What the hell do I tell the nurse?"

"Tell them I've gone to arrest a murderer. Tell them you're marrying a madman."

He stepped towards her. Grace took a step back. Shook her head. "No. I don't want you to kiss me. And don't tell me it'll be alright. Just go. Kiss me when it's over."

Ernie Moss looked up at him from the Christmas Eve paperwork.

'You mean it ruins your relationship?'

'No, son. You can leave that to the other 364 days of the year.'

Brady walked out of the door. Down the corridor. Past the nurses' station.

Knew he'd never had a choice.

29

"Tell me again," Tess said as he climbed into the car. "Simply. So I can convince Fitzpatrick I'm not a lunatic. So I can make some sort of token defence before I'm transferred to Blackpool."

"Blackpool?" Brady said. "I'll join you. I think my wedding was just called off."

Tess looked across at him. "No, it wasn't," she said. "Grace found out there'll be two of you married to the job. If she didn't already know."

Ignore the headache. Get this done. Go back to bed. Don't think about the look on Grace's face...

"Did you tell him?" Brady said.

"The boss? Of course I told him. He can't come back and find two different people in the cells for one murder."

"What did he say?"

"Not much. He's with the Chief Constable and the local politicians all day. He asked me what I thought. I said you'd convinced me. At least enough to get in the car."

"And bring some back-up."

"Right. And bring some back-up. Harvey and Elleray. The back-up boys..."

Tess overtook a line of stationary cars. Turned right at the lights. Checked the rear-view mirror.

"How long?" Brady asked.

"Until we get there? Fifteen minutes. Twenty if there's any traffic. We'll be alright. The removal men won't have turned up until eight."

"Did the boss say anything else?"

"You really want to know?"

"Yes."

"Four words. Don't fuck it up. Which you should take as a compliment. 'Don't fuck it up' means he sees something in you. And he trusts me to use my judgement. Fitz is under a lot of pressure. Crime figures. Chief Constable with an eye on his next promotion. Politicians who've never done a day's work in their lives but obviously know everything there is to know about being a copper. And it's Fitz's job to deliver."

"So don't fuck it up."

"Exactly."

THEY WERE on the dual carriageway now.

It can't be much further...

"Come on then," Tess said. "Run it all past me again. We need to work out how to play this."

"I had a lot of time to think," Brady said. "Awake all night, staring at the ceiling. Determined to get it right. For Stan. And – "

"There's plenty feel that way," Tess said. "But 'getting it right for Stan' means Gary Cooke getting life. So you're going out on a limb. *I'm* going out on a limb believing you."

"So don't fuck it up?"

"Exactly. Or it's Blackpool. In the winter."

"There was one question I couldn't answer," Brady said. "If Gary Cooke killed her, why did he kill her on Saturday night? Why *that* Saturday night? Then the other questions. Why did he park his car on the wrong side of the road? Why did he slam the door three times?"

"So that makes it Gilman?"

"If it's not Gary Cooke, who else can it be? You know the stats. We're murdered by people we know. And the brothers look enough alike. Especially on a wet night."

"All cats are grey in the dark?"

"All cats that are half-brothers."

"Why?" Tess said. "Why did he kill her? You haven't answered that."

"Revenge. Gary Cooke cheated him out of his share of the business. Gilman thought he was being paid. He wasn't. It was a loan. Cooke asked for the money two days after the funeral."

'Linda's not cold in the ground. And it's give him the shares or lose my house. Our house...'

"Something else," Tess said. "It's personal. She turned him down."

"We don't know that."

"New house? New start? I bet he thought, 'this is my chance.' She was sympathetic when his wife died. He wouldn't be the first man to mistake sympathy for attraction. Gradually the obsession grows. And remember what Angie said. 'If I can't have her no-one can?' No, we don't know. But I won't give you long odds..."

Brady nodded. "You're probably right. So he sees his chance. He's sold the house. He's going to Spain. If he can't have shares in the business he'll destroy the business. Gary can't sell cars if he's serving life."

"So he hires a Porsche?"

"He must have done."

"That won't be hard to trace. Not many places where you can hire a Porsche for the weekend."

"Right. So he parks. Makes sure Sarah sees him. Or hears him. Makes sure she's terrified. And she sees who she expects to see. Gary."

Tess turned off the dual carriageway. Brady recognised the parade of shops. She indicated and turned right. Checked the rear-view mirror again.

"Thanks, skip," Brady said. "Thanks for believing me."

Tess turned towards him. Raised her eyebrows. "Believe you? What makes you think I believe you? I just needed an excuse to avoid the paperwork. Fancied some fresh air... Anyway, we'll soon find out. There's the removal van."

30

A large white removal lorry, the back doors open, a ramp leading up to the back. A washing machine standing on the drive. 'Carpenter's Removals' on the side of the van in royal blue. The company slogan underneath it. *Moving you to a better life.*

Tess parked the car. Brady glanced in the wing mirror. Saw Harvey and Ellery park behind them.

"How do you want to play this, skip?"

Tess exhaled. Tapped her finger on the steering wheel. "I've been asking myself that all the way. We can't arrest him. We've no evidence. Selling your house and flying to Spain is hardly a criminal offence."

Brady didn't speak. He was waiting for her to reach the obvious conclusion. The only conclusion.

"Questioning?" Tess said, talking to herself more than to Brady. "On what grounds? Any competent solicitor would have him out by this afternoon. And sue us for a missed flight tomorrow morning. And Gary Cooke's solicitors would have a field day.

Grace's father's firm. I need to tell him. Once and for all...

"We've got to tip him over the edge," Brady said.

Tess stared through the windscreen. Started tapping the steering wheel again. Nodded to herself. "You knew this would happen didn't you? Knew it was the only way?"

"Yes." Brady's mouth was suddenly dry.

"So Fitz tells me not to fuck it up and my solution is to send you in on your own. Into a house where you've convinced me there's a murderer. Blackpool? Not a bloody chance. Bergen. If I'm lucky."

"I can do it," Brady said.

Tess didn't reply. She opened the car door. Walked back up the road. Brady twisted round. Saw her giving instructions to Eddie Harvey.

He looked across the road. Saw two men in royal blue overalls lift the washing machine into the back of the removal van. No sign of Darren Gilman.

Tess was back. "Five minutes," she said. "You've got five minutes to give us a reason to arrest him. The clock starts the minute you disappear up the drive."

"That's fine," Brady said. "Five minutes is fine. I'll find a way."

"Good. Because bluntly, Blackpool's a shit hole."

BRADY WALKED ACROSS THE ROAD. "Is Darren around?" he said to one of the removal men.

"Upstairs, mate. Tell him we're just on our break will you? We'll be in the van for ten minutes."

"No problem."

Yep, I've thought this through. Hadn't even worked out how I was going to get the removal men out of the way...

Brady walked up the drive. The front door was open.

No doormat with 'Welcome' on it. No Simon and Garfunkel...

He walked into the hall. The carpets were still down, clearly left for whoever was moving in. But the house was almost empty. He looked in the lounge. Two packing crates. *Carpenter's* stencilled on the side. Nothing else.

The carpet under the window still three shades lighter than the rest of the room.

One carpet the new owners won't be keeping...

The cat – definitely the thinnest cat he'd ever seen – was dozing in a patch of sunlight. "What's going to happen to you then, mate?"

"Hello?" Brady shouted upstairs.

"I'm up here," Gilman yelled. "Put those two packing crates in the van will you? And speed it up. I need to be out by eleven."

I think we can arrange that...

Brady walked slowly up the stairs.

Five minutes. It must be four by now.

He was in the main bedroom. Two pale blue walls. One wall papered. Darker blue, white flowers climbing up it. A mirrored wardrobe ran the length of the fourth wall. Gilman had one of the doors open. Checking he'd not left anything.

"Mr Gilman?"

"I said to you. Put the crates in the van. How many times – "

"Michael Brady. You might remember me. Detective Constable Brady. I saw you – "

Gilman slowly turned round. "Of course I fucking remember you. What the hell do you want? I'm moving. And who gave you permission to walk into my house?"

"The door was open. The removal men told me where I'd find you. There are a couple of questions I still need to ask you."

"You've arrested my brother for God's sake. What are you talking about?"

Three minutes now...

'The question they don't expect, Mike. Ask the obvious question and they've got the lie ready and waiting.'

"How long did you keep her clothes?"

"What?"

"Your wife's clothes. How long did you keep them?"

Brady saw it. Not on the same scale as his brother. Not yet. But the muscles tightening. The jaw clenching.

"Is that what you're here for? Some sort of sick joke? So you can laugh about it in the police canteen?"

Ignore his questions. Keep him off-guard. Provoke him...

"What are you doing about your cat?"

"What?"

"What are you doing about your cat? You're moving. I didn't see a cat basket downstairs."

Gilman took a pace towards him.

Almost as big as his brother. Not as athletic. But big enough...

"Fuck the cat. Some old woman will take her in. What

do you think I'm going to do? Take the fucking cat with me?"

"Did she cry?" Brady said.

Another pace closer. "What?"

"Did she cry? Sarah Cooke. When she realised you were going to kill her. Did she cry?"

Brady saw the effort it took. Gilman fought to control his temper. Consciously took a step back.

"I don't know what you're talking about."

You've no time left.

"Yes you do. Saturday night. You parked the Porsche across the road. Slammed the car door three times. Did you smile when she let you in? You must have held her. Slid your hand onto her throat…"

"You're making this up. You've arrested my brother."

"…That's when she realised isn't it? She hadn't noticed before. So relieved you weren't Gary. Then she felt your hand on her throat. Realised you were wearing gloves. A split-second of knowing before you started squeezing. So did she cry, Mr Gilman?"

Brady reached into his pocket. Pulled his mobile phone out. "Or shall I phone for back-up? Let the jury decide?"

Brady saw it. Muscles tightening. Fists clenching.

Now he's the same as his brother.

Out of control…

Gilman closed the gap in two strides. Swept his right hand into Brady's arm. Sent the mobile phone spinning through the air. Moved with surprising speed. Grabbed the front of Brady's jacket. Flung him across the room. Sprawling backwards into the mirrored doors.

Protect your head. Protect your head.

Brady flung an arm out to break his fall. Too late. Felt his head crash into the glass. Heard the glass shatter. Felt the splinters hitting his face. Felt the wave of dizziness wash over him.

Opened his eyes. Looked up.

Saw Gilman crouching over him.

Saw the shard of glass in his right hand.

"You fucking little prick. I should use this. Dump you in the wardrobe. Let you bleed out."

"New owners," Brady managed to say.

"They're not coming until this afternoon. I'll be in Spain."

"YOU WON'T. You're under arrest."

Gilman slowly straightened up. Inch by inch.

Turned round.

Brady looked past him. Saw Tess Knightly standing in the doorway.

"You won't, Gilman. You're under arrest for assaulting a police officer."

"Fuck you, bitch."

Gilman rushed towards her, the shard of glass raised.

Tess Knightly took a step back. Crouched slightly. Pivoted on her left leg. Spun round, her back to Gilman, hair streaming behind her. Pushed off with her left leg. Brought her right leg sweeping round while she was still in mid-air.

Her right foot struck Gilman on the side of his chin. Knocked him sideways. There was a split second when he stood, uncomprehending, staring at her. Then he sank to his knees.

Brady pushed himself upright. Shook his head. Knew he hadn't done any more damage.

Looked at Gilman. Looked at Tess Knightly.

"Bloody hell, skip. I thought you helped at the women's refuge in your spare time."

"I do," she said. "One night a week. Wednesday. Tuesdays and Thursdays I do kickboxing."

GILMAN WAS CUFFED and in the back of the patrol car. "We'll see you back at the station," Tess said to Eddie Harvey.

"Bit of a shock for the new owners," Brady said. "Find their dream house is a crime scene."

Tess unlocked the car. "Not for long. We won't find anything. All he did in there was sit and brood. Dwell on the past. And get bitter."

"And plan his revenge," Brady said.

"Yeah, that too. Let's get back. And Mike…"

"Skip?"

"That roundhouse kick. It never happened. You got up. Caught him with a lucky punch."

Brady nodded. "Yeah. Couldn't believe it when he went down…"

. . .

TESS STARTED THE CAR. There was a tap on the window. A man in royal blue overalls.

Break's over then...

She wound the window down.

"Hey, love. You've arrested him. What are we supposed to do now?"

"What were you supposed to do before?" Tess said.

"Putting all his stuff in storage."

Tess pursed her lips. Made a decision. "Do that," she said. "With what you've got in the van. Our guys will want to look at it. The rest of it, leave it. Don't go in the house again. And the stuff you put in storage..."

"Yes, love?"

"You can book it in for about twenty years."

31

"It didn't take long, Darren," Fitzpatrick said. "Half an hour's checking. A garage in Leeds. One Porsche, hired for the weekend."

"You don't have to say anything." The duty solicitor placed a cautionary hand on Gilman's arm. Michael Brady, standing behind the one-way window – watching, listening and learning – saw him shrug her off.

"I'm done," he said. "The sunshine would have been nice. But I've done enough. Fucked him. Fucked his business."

"The Porsche," Fitzpatrick said. "Why go to Leeds?"

"Because I couldn't risk Gary finding out could I? He knows all the Porsche dealers in Manchester. So it was a bloody train ride to Leeds."

Fitzpatrick sighed. Looked at Tess Knightly out of the corner of his eye. "We're about to charge you with murder, Darren. An hour on Trans-Pennine Express is going to be the least of your worries. But do me one favour. Tell me where you got the number plates made. We like to help our colleagues in West Yorkshire."

Gilman laughed. "That was easy. Little place round the back of the garage. Told them I didn't have a log book 'cos the car was a present for the wife. And cash always talks doesn't it?"

"So you drove to Sarah Cooke's house. Parked the car outside – "

"Across the road. Just in case she was upstairs."

Brady turned to Eddie Harvey next to him. "Gilman's enjoying himself. Starting to show off."

"This is how the boss does it. They think he's a simple copper. They're just having a chat. By the time Fitz has finished they've confessed to the crime, the Great Train Robbery and the Ripper murders."

"How did you make sure Sarah Cooke saw the car?" Tess said.

"Christ, you coppers are dim, aren't you? Gary always said you were. I know she's up 'cos the lights are on. So I just slam the door a few times. I know her. She's edgy. Nervous. That's going to make her look outside."

Fitzpatrick nodded. "And when she does that she's terrified..."

Gilman smiled and nodded.

"So terrified she's not thinking straight," Tess said. "How did you get her to open the door?"

"Fuck me, that's a tough one. I knocked. Because she thinks it's Gary. And she knows if she doesn't open the door he'll put his foot through it."

"How did you explain Gary's car?"

Gilman sighed theatrically. "He's lent it to me for the

weekend. We're mates again. Truth be told it isn't the exact same shade. But she can't tell in the dark. And she's shaking with terror. She can't think. I could have told her Elvis had given me the car. She's so relieved it's not Gary she'll believe anything."

"What did you say to her? She must have said, 'Why are you here?' Eleven o'clock on Saturday night?"

"Told her that I'd just had a feeling. A message from Linda. They went to a – what do you call them? Spiritualist – when Sarah's mother died. Before Linda got ill. Didn't she tell you that? Well, no reason why she should. But she believed in all that crap."

"And the more terrified she is the more she trusts you..." Jim Fitzpatrick shook his head. "I've a niece the same age..."

"And so you go into the lounge with her," Tess said. "Did you want to have sex with her? Was that it, Darren? She was so grateful, so relieved, so frightened that she asks you to stay?"

Gilman stared at her. Brady saw the muscles tighten again. Not quite Gary's red mist this time. But from the same family...

"That's none of your fucking business. I wanted to kill her. Fuck my brother. Pay him back. And I've done that. 'His brother's a murderer.' No-one's going to buy a car off him now."

"So you strangled her?"

Gilman relaxed. Sat back in his chair. Smiled again. "She was showing me a picture of her little girl. I told her she needed a hug first. Simple as that. One hand at the front, one at the back. She died while they were singing *Sound of Silence*. Fitting, don't you think?"

Jim Fitzpatrick turned. Look towards the window at where he knew Brady would be standing.

Gilman followed his gaze. Realised that Fitzpatrick was looking at someone. Realised who it must be. "No," he said, looking directly at Brady. "No, she didn't cry."

Jim Fitzpatrick turned back to Gilman.

"Darren Anthony Gilman, we are charging you…"

BRADY TURNED TO GO. Eddie Harvey followed him out of the door. "What next?" Harvey said. "You're the blue-eyed boy now, mate."

"I don't know. Whatever the boss tells me, I guess. I don't even know who I'll be working with."

"Are you going to the funeral?"

Brady shook his head. "I thought I should. But Tess told me not to. Says Stan's wife doesn't want it turning into a police funeral. Just her and the boss. And Ernie Moss – he'd known Stan since they trained together. I – "

Brady stopped. Two men were walking down the corridor towards them. One about his own age. In a suit. Who may as well have had 'ambitious solicitor' tattooed on his forehead. And a slightly dishevelled – but very cheerful – Gary Cooke. Looking even bigger in the confines of the corridor than he'd looked in the alley.

"Brady," he said. "I was wondering if I'd see you."

The solicitor took his arm. Tried to get him to walk past. "Come on, Gary."

Cooke shook him off as easily as he'd shoved Stan

Bulman to one side. "Just relax, Paul. All I'm doing is saying hello to Mr Brady. And I suppose I should say 'thank you.' I understand you're the towering intellect who worked it out. Mind you, it's a fucking low bar in this place."

Brady looked back at him. "Like I said in the alley. It's my job."

Cooke nodded. "Maybe it is. But let me give you some advice, son. Just make sure it's your job to come nowhere near me for the rest of your career. I owe you. And I don't forget."

Brady held his gaze.

I could do it. Right here. In front of witnesses. Push him too far. But I've got Grace to go home to...

"Have a good evening, Mr Cooke. Thanks for the advice. I'll keep it in mind."

32

"We got there in the end," Jim Fitzpatrick said.

Brady and Tess Knightly sat opposite him. Neither of them spoke.

"I'm impressed," he said to Brady. "Well done. For hanging on to Gary Cooke. And then having the insight to realise you'd hung on to the wrong man." He turned to Tess. "And it's a useful reminder – especially for me. Just because someone ticks all the boxes it doesn't mean they're guilty. So that's the good news."

So what's the bad news? We arrested the right man...

"Now the bad news. Gary Cooke's solicitors are going to be all over us like a rash. Wrongful arrest. Damage to his business. 'Blundering police wrongly arrest local businessman.' Right result: wrong headlines. As no doubt the Chief Constable will point out to me."

"You've fought bigger battles, boss," Tess said. "And won."

Fitzpatrick laughed. "And I'll fight them again. You sure you want this, Mike? The further up the ladder you go the more it's politics, the less it's policing. And there's more money in defending Gary Cooke than there is in arresting him. A lot more."

Brady nodded. "Yes, sir. I'm sure."

"Good, because now we come to the really bad news. Tess, give us five minutes will you?"

She nodded. Got up. Closed the door quietly behind her.

"Three weeks," Fitzpatrick said. "Three weeks since you sat in that chair and I sent you out with Stan Bulman."

'I'm on patrol with Eddie Harvey.'

'You were. You're not now. Detective Chief Inspector Fitzpatrick would like a word with you. So straighten your tie and two-at-a-time up those stairs. You've been called to God's right hand.'

"By any standards it's been eventful. Three weeks and you've walked into a crime scene without any back-up. Like I said, I don't like stupid coppers on my team, and that was stupid. Then you redeem yourself by clinging on to Gary Cooke. But then you walk out of the hospital." Fitzpatrick shook his head. "Even more stupid."

Brady knew he wasn't supposed to reply.

"But thanks to you we got the right result..." Fitzpatrick took a deep breath. Looked out of the window. Confirming the decision he'd already made...

It didn't take long.

"I'm not paid to be right all the time, Mike. I *am* paid to make tough decisions. There's obviously a vacancy in plain clothes. It was yours... but I'm giving it to Eddie Harvey. I'm putting you back in uniform."

Saturday night drunks. I don't know if I can go back to it. And I've failed. Failed in front of Grace. And her father...

Brady found the courage to speak. "Can I ask how long for, sir?"

"Until there's another vacancy, Mike."

"With respect, sir, I thought Bill Slater – "

"Was taking early retirement? He's changed his mind. Personal reasons."

"Yes, sir. Boss, I mean..."

Fitzpatrick looked at him. "You're entitled to know the reason why. You've got to go home to Grace. Tell her you're back in uniform. The reason's simple, Mike. I'm managing a team. Not a collection of individuals. Everyone knows what you did. You're brave, and you're intelligent. But you acted on your own. You do that again and it could get you – or someone else – into trouble. I can't be seen to ignore that. Or show favouritism. So that's my decision. And one day – ten, fifteen years down the line – there'll be a young copper opposite you. And you'll make the same decision."

Brady stood up. Tried not to show any emotion. Put his hand on the door handle.

"One last thing," Fitzpatrick said.

"Yes, boss?"

"Go and see the doctor. You're still not right. Get yourself signed off for a fortnight. That's an order. Get yourself better. And use the time to think about what I've said. You won't be in uniform for ever. Ask Tessa to come in will you?"

. . .

"You FANCY A BEER?" Tess had been with Fitzpatrick for less than five minutes. "A quick one before you break the bad news to Grace?"

"Did he tell you?"

"No, it's written all over your face."

Ten minutes later she walked back to their table with two bottles of Peroni. "Cheers," she said. "And he had no choice. If it makes you feel any better, I got a bollocking as well."

"For letting me go in on my own?"

"More or less. Like I said, he's under a lot of pressure. But he'd have been under a lot more pressure if Gary Cooke had gone to trial. Fitz knows that. You won't be in uniform for too long."

"Gary Cooke knew," Brady said. "He knew it was Gilman all the time."

Tess nodded. "Yeah, I think you're right."

"That was the other thing I realised in hospital. Gilman had done him a favour. They were still negotiating the financial settlement from the divorce. He didn't screw his brother: he helped him. Gary Cooke was taking the piss. I think he knew Gilman was going to Spain. Happy to sit in a cell until Gilman touched down. Figured he owed him that much.

"Before he phoned his solicitor? Fitz was right. There's a lot more money in defending him. Way more. Did you see the one that came to spring Gary Cooke? He was only your age. Sharp suit. Not one you'd buy on a copper's wages. You're not tempted?"

Brady nodded. "I did see. And no, I'm not. I'll serve my time. Go back in uniform. This is who I am."

Tess finished her beer.

"You want another one?" Brady asked.

"Yes, I do. But you need to go home to Grace. What are you going to tell her?"

Brady shrugged. "The truth. What else can I tell her?"

"Take care of her. And take care of yourself. Enjoy your two weeks off. It's like Angie said about abuse. Being a copper's the same. The scars don't show."

Brady stood up. "I'll see you in two weeks, I guess."

"You will." She hesitated. "Mike…"

"Yes, skip?"

"There's a proverb. It's Indian. Or Japanese. Every bloody proverb is Indian or Japanese. 'If you sit by the river long enough the body of your enemy will float past.' Well, you're a copper, so you don't have time to sit by the river. And you're in Manchester, so it's a canal. But it's a small town. Gary Cooke will float past sooner or later. And he won't have forgotten you."

Brady nodded. "Don't worry. He's already told me."

33

Brady put his key in the lock. Realised he hadn't had time to phone her all day. Wasn't sure where he was going to start with explanations. Screwed his eyes shut. Willed the headache away.

The first thing he noticed was the smell. Something good coming from the kitchen. He hung his coat up. Walked through the dining room. Grace had her back to him. Blue jeans, the rugby shirt she'd peeled off.

A lifetime ago...

"Are you making enough for two?"

She didn't turn round. "Of course I am. Puttanesca. Home-made. And home-made garlic bread."

"You can turn round," Brady said. "I'm not injured. A headache. I need you to take me to the doctor's in the morning. Nothing else."

She placed the wooden spoon across the top of the pan. Turned round slowly. Blinked away tears. Smiled. "I smell of garlic. And anchovies."

Brady smiled back. "I smell of beer."

He took two steps towards her. Wrapped his arms round her. Held her. "I love you, Grace," he said. "And I'm sorry. Truly sorry. But..."

She stepped back. "But what?"

"But the sauce is boiling."

"You bastard!" She picked up the wooden spoon. Threatened to hit him with it. Brady threw his left arm up to protect himself. She grabbed the garlic press off the worktop. Hit him with that instead.

Put her weapons down. Wrapped her arms round his neck. Kissed him hard.

"I love you too. But you do smell of beer. And smoke. What were you doing in the pub anyway?"

"Having a drink with Tess. She was giving me careers advice. Asking me if I was going to quit. Go shopping for suits and stripy ties."

"And are you?"

Brady shook his head. "No, I'm not."

"Good. Because I wouldn't marry a man who gave up. Now go and have a shower. I'm not taking you to bed smelling like that."

"I'm supposed to be convalescing for two weeks. Then..."

"What?"

'The truth. What else can I tell her?'

"I'm sorry. I'm back in uniform. At least until Bill Slater retires."

"Why?"

"Because I'm not a team player. That's why Tess was asking me – "

She put her hand on his cheek. Looked into his eyes. "You're on my team. That's all I care about."

"What about your father?"

"He's not marrying you, Michael. I am. And if I could do it tomorrow I would. Now go and get in the shower. No, on second thoughts go to the corner shop. I forgot the wine."

BRADY KISSED HER AGAIN. Then he went back into the hall, reached for his coat and walked out into the Manchester rain.

He saw the wet tarmac glistening. Looked up at the rain swirling in the streetlights.

Just like Saturday night. And there'll be plenty more nights like it...

His phone was ringing.

Brady glanced down at the display and smiled.

Grace's father.

Fed up with waiting for an answer. 'Have you seen sense or not, Mike?'

'Yes, I have seen sense.'

Police Constable Michael Brady pressed the green button.

Time to tell him the good news...

REVIEWS & FUTURE WRITING PLANS

Thank you for reading *The Scars Don't Show*. I really hope you enjoyed it.

If you did, could I ask a favour? Would you please review the book on Amazon? The **link to do that is here**: https://storyoriginapp.com/universalbooklinks/f0d4a226-737f-11eb-961e-8f472f259d02

Reviews are important to me for three reasons. First of all, good reviews help to sell the book. Secondly, there are some review and book promotion sites that will only look at a book if it has a certain number of reviews and/or a certain ratio of 5* reviews. And lastly, reviews are useful feedback.

So I'd appreciate you taking five minutes to leave a review and thank you in advance to anyone who does so.

What next?

This is the first book in the Michael Brady Short Reads series, following two full-length novels.

Next on my list is the third full-length book, which will be set in Whitby in the early months of 2016.

That will be followed by the second Short Read, looking back at another pivotal case in Brady's early career.

I'm aiming to have both those books out by July/August of this year.

If you'd like to receive regular updates on my writing – and previews of these books – you can join my mailing list by clicking this link: https://www.subscribepage.com/markrichards

Alternatively you can follow me on Amazon, or join my Reader Group on Facebook: just look for 'Mark Richards: Writer' on Facebook and ask to join.

THE MICHAEL BRADY BOOKS

Salt in the Wounds

His best friend has been murdered, his daughter's in danger.

There's only one answer. Going back to his old life.

The one that cost him his wife...

'Salt in the Wounds' is available on Amazon.

"Had me gripped from the start. A truly captivating story, very well told. Really didn't want it to end and eagerly awaiting the next one."

"Fabulous! Had me gripped from start to finish. Reminded me of Mark Billingham's detective, Tom Thorne."

"You know you're hooked when you care what happens to the characters. Loved Brady, Ash and Frankie. Can't wait for the rest of the series."

"Loved everything about this book. A gripping plot with unexpected twists and turns. Believable characters that you feel you really know by the last page. I could smell the sea air in Whitby..."

The River Runs Deep

Good people do bad things

    Bad people do good things

    Sometimes it's hard to tell the difference...

'The River Runs Deep' is available on Amazon. Like 'Salt in the Wounds,' it's on the Kindle and in paperback, with an audiobook due to follow later this year.

"That's the trouble with a really good book – you want to keep reading but you don't want it to end. Loved the natural dialogue: witty and believable."

"Book 2 of the Michael Brady series, and it's every bit as good as the first. Read it in three sittings – but only because real life got in the way!"

"This book made me question myself. How far would I go to protect my own family?"

"I read a lot of detective books, but none has drawn me into another world like this one. Loved it. Cannot wait for the rest of the series."

"Another thrilling read. Could not put it down! The depth of the characters is so good I couldn't stop thinking about the story after I'd finished it."

ABOUT ME

I've been writing full-time since 2010, when I sold my business in financial services, sent my stripy ties to the charity shop and – as one client put it – 'ran away to join the circus.'

My time is now split between copywriting for my clients and writing my own books. You can find details of all the books on my website – www.markrichards.co.uk – or on my Amazon author page.

I live in Scarborough, on the Yorkshire Coast. Whitby – where the full-length Michael Brady books are set – is 20 miles up the road. I thought I knew Whitby quite well – but you don't realise how little you know about a town until you start planning a murder...

ACKNOWLEDGMENTS

As always, a number of people helped me with the book. Let me start by thanking the members of my Reader Group on Facebook for their support, encouragement and constructive criticism. I'd especially like to thank those members of the Group who proof-read the book for me: I cannot tell you how much I appreciated your diligence and attention to detail.

I'd also like to thank the serving and retired police officers in the UK who helped with the book. The small details they corrected and the suggestions they made has, unquestionably, produced a better book.

As always I must thank my wife, Beverley, for her support and understanding – and for not rolling her eyes too much when she said, "What are you going to do now this one's finished?" And I said, "Start the next one…"

Mark Richards

March 2021

Printed in Great Britain
by Amazon